SYMPATHY FOR A STRANGER

BROTHERHOOD PROTECTORS WORLD

KATE MCKEEVER

SYMPATHY FOR A STRANGER

SHADOW OPS SERIES

KATE MCKEEVER

Copyright © 2021, Kate McKeever

This book is a work of fiction. Names, characters, places and incidents are products of the author's imagination or used fictitiously. Any resemblance to actual events, locales or persons living or dead is entirely coincidental.

© 2021 Twisted Page Press, LLC ALL RIGHTS RESERVED

No part of this book may be used, stored, reproduced or transmitted without written permission from the publisher except for brief quotations for review purposes as permitted by law.

This book is licensed for your personal enjoyment only. This book may not be re-sold or given away to other people. If you would like to share this book with another person, please purchase an additional copy for each recipient. If you're reading this book and did not purchase it, or it was not purchased for your use only, please purchase your own copy.

My books are always dedicated to my parents. The memories of their thirst for knowledge and drive are always with me.

BROTHERHOOD PROTECTORS
ORIGINAL SERIES BY ELLE JAMES

Brotherhood Protectors Series
Montana SEAL (#1)
Bride Protector SEAL (#2)
Montana D-Force (#3)
Cowboy D-Force (#4)
Montana Ranger (#5)
Montana Dog Soldier (#6)
Montana SEAL Daddy (#7)
Montana Ranger's Wedding Vow (#8)
Montana SEAL Undercover Daddy (#9)
Cape Cod SEAL Rescue (#10)
Montana SEAL Friendly Fire (#11)
Montana SEAL's Mail-Order Bride (#12)
SEAL Justice (#13)
Ranger Creed (#14)
Delta Force Rescue (#15)
Dog Days of Christmas (#16)
Montana Rescue (Sleeper SEAL)
Hot SEAL Salty Dog (SEALs in Paradise)
Hot SEAL Hawaiian Nights (SEALs in Paradise)

Hot SEAL Bachelor Party (SEALs in Paradise)

CHAPTER 1

Dust floated around her in tiny particles of color against the bright sky above. Lacey wondered idly why she was lying so awkwardly and why she didn't feel relaxed on this beautiful day. Her back ached something awful and a weird squealing was making her ears ring. She turned her head to see what the source of the noise was and all came rushing back to her.

"Davey! Baby!" She struggled against the mass of plastic enveloping her, blinding her. Pushing at the airbag, she squirmed against the restraint from the tightened seat belt and tried to crane her neck to view the back seat.

Her son, her tiny, tiny son, was lying in the car seat, slightly askew where the impact had pushed at the anchors and, thankfully crying, red-faced and terrified. "It's okay, honey. Mommy's here. Mommy's here."

Thanking God Davey could cry but tamping down panic her son might be injured, Lacey reached to release her seat belt only to cry out at the pain in her shoulder. She took a deep breath, tamping down sudden nausea, and pushed again at the deflated airbag.

A face appeared in the passenger side window, a man.

"Help. My son is in the back seat and I can't release my seat belt." She pleaded, only to gasp when he lifted a pistol and pointed it at her. The last thing she saw was the narrow pipe that made up the pistol's barrel and the black void that the opening presented.

Minutes, hours later she awakened in a hospital room, pain radiating everywhere and her mind muzzy. "Davey! my baby?"

"Shh. It's okay. You're going to be fine."

"Where's my son? I need to see my son," Lacey struggled to move despite the pain radiating from her side and her left arm but found herself held down. A woman in scrubs called for help over her shoulder. "We need to get her calm. She'll ruin all the work the doc did." Soon afterward, Lacey fell into a drugged sleep, but one rife with dreams.

Dreams of her son sitting in his car seat, screaming. Dreams of the flash of a gun and pain. Dreams of a man unbuckling the seat and taking her son.

The next time she awoke, it was with a scream. Lacey tried to sit up only to groan in pain and flop back on the mattress.

"Easy. Don't move too fast." A nurse appeared at her side and laid a hand on her shoulder, which felt numb and sore at the same time.

"Where's my son? He was in the back seat."

A frown crossed the nurse's face then she turned her head and spoke low to another, unseen person. When she turned back to Lacey, she said, "There's someone here to talk to you."

Lacey felt her blood turn to ice. "Where's Davey? Where's my son?"

A man dressed in a neat shirt and tie with a blazer came to stand by her bed. "Ms. Burke? I'm Detective Branson with the Seattle PD. Do you feel up to answering a few questions?"

"Not until you tell me where my son is." Her voice, high and shrill, surprised her but Lacey didn't care. An alarm rang near her bed and the nurse approached again. "She's getting too agitated, Detective. You need to either calm her down or leave."

"No! I want to know where Davey is!" She rose, her need for information greater than the pain radiating over her body. The detective and nurse both reached for her and flattened her on the bed. He spoke firmly. "Quieten down and I'll tell you."

She shuddered a breath, sure he was going to tell her Davey was in the care of a social worker or hospital personnel. Instead, he perched on a stool near the bed and stared into her eyes. "There wasn't a child in the car."

Lacey started crying, great jagged howls of pain. "My son! They've taken my son."

The detective didn't stay much longer. Any questions he wanted to ask were drowned in a pool of misery, panic, and terror. Lacey cried, screamed her son's name, only to drop off into an uneasy sleep after the nurse administered a sedative.

CELIE GARCIA WOKE at the sound of a phone trilling near her ear. She nudged Saint in the side, "Your turn."

He moaned and reached over her to pluck the phone from its place on the charging pad. "Lo."

He paused a moment then passed it to her. "It's for you."

Celie glanced at the clock display on the nightstand. Two in the morning. Either her dad was ill or Hank had an emergency assignment for them. Seeing as Hank could give the assignment to either her or Saint, it had to be personal. Her sleep fog dissipated in an instant and she held the receiver to her ear. "Celie speaking."

"Ms. Garcia? Celie Garcia?" The voice wasn't familiar, so it wasn't Maggie, her dad's girlfriend. Celie heaved a sigh and replied in the affirmative. "What can I do for you?" At two o'clock in the blessed morning.

"We have a woman in the hospital and she doesn't have any next of kin listed. She did have your name in her ICE notification, though."

ICE, or in case of emergency, was an old but effective way of making personal information available, in the event of emergencies. Celie frowned. Was it Maggie? She was the only person, other than her father that might have that information, though that was a fine line as well. Maggie had relatives in the same neighborhood she lived in.

"Who is the woman?" Celie asked as she met Saint's eyes. Her lover, intent and focused now that they were both awake, stood and dressed in a pair of sweatpants. Celie watched him retrieve the prosthetic arm he'd left on to charge for the night. He didn't take his eyes from her as he started the familiar process of donning the device.

"Lacey Burke."

"Who?" She searched her memory, trying to recall anyone in the army, her old neighborhood, anywhere, with that name. She came up empty.

The person repeated the name and then continued. "She could use a friend or relative right now."

"Is she seriously hurt?"

"We can't release that kind of information without her signed consent. As a matter of fact, I'm kinda crossing the line by calling you."

"So why are you?" Celie stood and accepted the pants and t-shirt Saint held out to her and started dressing.

"I'm her nurse for the night. She's been agitated the entire time and needs someone who can look after her. I can't tell you much more, not without her permission and she's under sedation right now." A short pause followed, as if the nurse was trying to come to a decision. "I think she may be in trouble."

Celie followed up with some questions regarding where Lacey Burke was, in Seattle of all places, and what hospital they were to go to. After a couple more calls and a quick shower and packing, she and Saint headed to Bozeman and the airport.

"Think she's looking for the Brotherhood?" Saint asked as he pulled into short term parking at the airport.

"Maybe," Celie responded as she stared into the dusky night, artificially lit with lights in the lot. But she wondered, deep inside if there was another reason Lacey Burke had her name. Somehow, she didn't think it was the Brotherhood that was the connection. Why she didn't know, but she wondered if this was going to permanently alter her life, just as the man sitting beside her had.

THE ROOM at the end of the hall was dimly lit from the inside, making the predawn light both welcoming and eerie. Celie stepped into the room just as a nurse came around the bed. "Celie?" she whispered and Celie nodded.

"She's been asleep since before I called you." The nurse smoothed the sheet over the still woman's form. A heavily wrapped shoulder lay atop the covers and her face was splotched with bruises, including what looked like a couple of black eyes. Celie wondered if she'd been in a car accident.

"Do you think she'll wake soon?"

"Probably, the sedative wasn't terribly strong but enough to quiet her and put her into a deep sleep for a few hours. I hope seeing you will help keep her calm." The nurse nodded toward a couple of chairs and then left the room with one last look at monitors ranged beside the bed.

Celie approached the woman, trying in vain to bring up memories of her. Nothing. The light blonde hair, straight and a bit stained from the blood and what looked like dust, lay against the pillow and over her slim shoulders. Her face, pale and wan, had no recognizable feature other than a perfectly straight nose that Celie might have envied in another time. Now, she only felt sympathy for the stranger.

Less than an hour later, Lacey began to toss her head and murmur a name. Celie sat straighter in the uncomfortable chair alongside the bed. As she leaned forward, Lacey cried out, "Davey!"

Celie stood and held her hand out, almost afraid to touch the woman. Lacey Burke's pale gray eyes held panic and terror. She darted looks around the room finally landing on Celie. Her panting breaths stopped abruptly and she stared intently into Celie's eyes.

"You're Celie, aren't you? Tony's sister."

Celie started. Her brother had been her closest friend and confidante until his death a little over two years ago. "I am. How did you know Tony?"

Lacey closed her eyes, "We dated."

"And he gave you my name?" Celie felt Saint come to her side and she quietly reached for his hand.

"No. I found that out myself. After his death." Lacey opened her eyes again and said quietly. "I'm so sorry about his death."

Celie swallowed against the pain. Two years weren't long enough to erase her brother's memory or the connection they'd had. And she'd never forgive the man who'd taken his life, even if the bastard was dead. "If you dated, it must have been hard on you too."

"We didn't know each other long." Lacey's eyes filled and she lifted her head up to stare at the ceiling. "We dated for a couple of months, then we kinda had a falling out."

Celie waited. There was something else, she knew. Why else would this woman have her name as a contact? She let the silence reign for a few minutes then, as she was about to question Lacey, the young woman turned her eyes back on Celie and Saint.

"I had a baby. Tony was the father."

Celie felt her knees go wobbly for an instant and she immediately called on her training to keep a blank face and firm stance. Saint's hand tightened on hers. "Did Tony know?" And why the hell hadn't he told her and Dad, if he had.

Lacey nodded, "That was the reason we fought. I told him, just to let him know. I wasn't intending for him to have any responsibilities. But he wanted to get married." Lacey sighed and started to fiddle with the edge of the sheet at her waist. "I refused him. We didn't know each other that well, not well enough to get married, at any rate. He got angry and we'd not talked for about a week. I called only to get a message that the voice mail was full. I figured he just didn't want to talk to me. I only found out about his death when I saw it online."

"So, you didn't plan on telling his family about the baby?" Celie's anger came through clearly in her question.

Lacey stared her down. "I hadn't really thought about it after Tony died. I spent most of the time between then and when Davey came getting prepared for his birth. Afterwards, life and stuff interfered."

"So why now? Why are you carrying my name in your emergency contacts?"

Lacey's expression turned haunted again and she blurted. "Because someone is trying to kill me and I think they've taken my son."

CHAPTER 2

KYLE STRETCHED as he resumed his stance against his sparring partner. Rachel, lithe and lean, was the newest addition to the Shadow Ops organization and out to prove she was as good as any man around. So far, he'd thrown her four times and she was still getting up for more.

"You sure you want to go again?" He asked even as she advanced, her eyes full of what looked a lot like anger.

"Hell, yeah." She swung at him then threw a leg out in a kick that, if it had connected, would have sent him into a painful tailspin, seeing as it was aimed at his crotch. Instead, he stepped to the side and sent her down with another blow to her side. He'd learned the hard way not to pull his punches with this one.

"Damn it!" she muttered and recovered her

stance, then pulled back when a phone trilled. They both turned to the bench along the side of the room and Kyle retrieved his cell phone, glancing at the text. "It's me."

She nodded and headed to the other bench where towels were stacked in neat, white order. Grabbing two, she returned and handed him one as he read the message.

"We'll have to continue this another day, Payne. I've gotta report to the boss."

She gave another nod, relief sharp in her eyes.

Kyle strode to the office, not bothering to change out of his workout clothes. The text, short and to the point, as usual, was one he'd not seen before. "New assignment asap."

He knocked on the closed office door and at the command, entered. Kyle quelled the urge to salute. He might have been out of the military for almost six years but the man before him still engendered the same level of respect and, to be frank, awe.

Kane Reynolds sat at the battered wooden desk, an opened folder the only thing cluttering the surface, other than a framed picture that faced away from anyone entering the room. He glanced up then gestured to a chair. "Have a seat. We need to go over a couple of things before you head out."

Kyle nodded and relaxed slightly, aware he'd been in a ready position all the while. He sat then leaned forward. Another mission. Another chance to get rid of the excess energy that zinged through him when he was off the field.

"There's a woman who needs a covert bodyguard."

"But I don't do bodyguarding." Kyle's pulse calmed, the thrum of excitement fading with each breath.

"You're the one needed for this assignment. She's in danger and has had her son kidnapped. Time is of the essence to find the kidnappers as well as to keep her out of the line of fire." Kane glanced up from the file he'd been reviewing. "She's been shot and stabbed, as well as forced off the road in less than six months. She's not got a lot of chances left."

"And my expertise?" Kyle was not known for being a soft and reassuring guard dog for people. His talents lie in hiding in the dark and killing people as quickly and quietly as possible. The army had taught him and used his natural talents to the fullest extent. The only thing they hadn't taught him was how to leave the service and live life as a civilian.

"That's one of the reasons I'm assigning you to this woman. Apparently, she doesn't know who is targeting her or why." At Kyle's scoff, Kane frowned and continued. "I know. But from what Hank Patterson is telling me, she's a reliable source. It's up to you to find who is trying to kill her. Hank and his team will try to find out why."

Kyle nodded, his mind already racing to detail the tools and weapons he'd need to fulfill his mission. "Where is she?"

"Seattle. She's in the hospital, should be discharged in a few days. You'll be there to cover her."

"And after she's released?"

Kane stared into space for a moment then returned his gaze to Kyle. "You find the bastard who took her son and retrieve him."

THE FLIGHT from Georgia to Montana wasn't nearly long enough for Kyle to relax and too short to take advantage of the woman seated in the seat next to him. He'd used the excess energy he always had flowing through him before a mission to his advantage by flirting. She'd been a little reticent at first but, given time, he'd have had her before the plane landed. As it was, she'd hinted broadly that he partake of her company-paid hotel room, as well as a steak dinner.

He carried her case off the plane, gently turning down her invitation for drinks. After all, he had the mission ahead of him, he didn't need the distraction the pretty brunette had offered now that the plane had landed.

The hospital, bustling as every other medical place he'd been to, offered another set of obstacles to cross. Kyle found the correct floor and then the right room in minutes. Once he stepped into the room, however, he found a couple of hurdles he hadn't planned on.

The dark man standing between him and the women in the room looked familiar. Tall, with military seeping from every pore, the guy stood braced against the enemy. His left arm hung at his side and ended in a gloved hand while his right rested on his waist. If he didn't have a pistol on him, Kyle knew there was another equally dangerous weapon concealed on the man.

"Shadow?" He questioned Kyle and then, at Kyle's sharp nod, he extended a hand.

"Luc Benatou, Saint. Brotherhood." He gestured into the room. "My partner Celie Garcia." The dark, curly-haired woman standing protectively at the bedside nodded, and then Kyle's eyes turned to the woman lying in the bed and inhaled.

She was probably pretty, he mused, if she hadn't gotten punched by a brute or an equally unrepentant airbag. She had two black eyes and the pale gray of her irises were rimmed with red from the impact. Her face sported several scratches and a couple of dark bruises along her jawline. She had bandages on an arm and, from his report, along her side as well, where she'd been grazed by a bullet. He returned his gaze to her face. Her eyes, her haunted gray eyes held him and he fell. Fell for the woman he realized he'd do anything for. Anything to remove that pain and fear.

Kyle approached her slowly and then stood at her bedside. "Have you been told about me?"

She nodded and took a deep breath. "I was told you'd protect me and find the kidnapper. I don't care about me." She looked at him intently, as if memorizing his face. "Just find my son."

Saint and Celie could have been in the next room for all he knew. Kyle seated himself in the chair that ranged beside the bed and asked Lacey for information.

"I started having problems about a year ago." She said. "My apartment was broken into, my car vandalized. I moved from LA to Seattle, thinking I'd move to a better place to raise Davey, my son." She shook her head. "I was okay for a couple months then it started again. "I had weird notes shoved under the wiper of my car. Then another break-in and I got mugged. The police said it was a mugging, anyway. I don't think so." She raised her brimming eyes to the ceiling and sighed. "I should have moved someplace else. Anywhere else."

"Do you know why someone would be trying to hurt you?" Kyle asked gently, forcing himself to stay where he was rather than enfolding her in his embrace.

"No!" She wailed and then visibly calmed herself. "No. I worked in costume design in LA and got a similar job in a theater in Seattle. I don't have secrets. I don't take chances, I never have."

"No drugs, no loans you couldn't pay off?" He continued and got a glare from her in response.

"I said no. I don't even drink regularly. I tried pot once in high school and hated the lack of control I had so I never tried anything again. I only have a car loan." She paused, then continued, "Nothing."

Saint stepped forward and folded his arms over his chest. In that instance, Kyle remembered him. He'd been at a house that Kyle had been hired to surveil a few months ago. The situation had gotten a little interesting but nothing the team, including the Brotherhood representative, couldn't handle. His view of the guy went up in respect.

He glanced over his shoulder at Lacey. Her eyes remained on him and her expression was one of possible hope. He smiled slightly at her. "We have some things to go over, Lacey. Do you feel up to it?"

She nodded and shifted slightly in the bed. Celie adjusted a pillow and lifted the head of the bed before both women seemed satisfied with the result. Lacey turned a steady gaze to Kyle. "Tell me about yourself. Who you work for, what your expertise is. I don't want someone around that isn't going to be able to deal with the consequences."

"What consequences?" Detective Branson stood at the edge of the room. He let the door swing shut and advanced, taking in the others. "I guess I'm a little late for the party."

Kyle met him halfway into the room and halted him with a look and wide stance. "I'm Ms. Burke's security. Can I help you?"

"It's okay, Kyle. This is the police detective that was here earlier. Come on in, Detective," Lacey said and Kyle moved to stand near her bed. The detective sent him a look and then pulled a note pad from his jacket pocket and stood at the periphery of the group. "I needed to ask you some questions, now that you're a little more—"

"Calm?" Lacey responded sarcastically. "I'm not calm, Detective. I'm worried and I'm terrified I'll never see my son again. And I'm fairly confident you didn't believe me when I told you he'd been kidnapped earlier."

"Why do you need security, Ms. Burke?" He shot back, ignoring her reference to her son.

"Because she has been in at least three situations where her life has been threatened or she has been injured. You want the list?" Celie stepped forward, her face flushed and Kyle noted Saint covering her back immediately.

He knew some of the story, but he needed to hear it from another source, so Kyle didn't intervene. Instead, he stepped closer to Lacey and watched the interview unfold.

Celie held up one finger, "Lacey's apartment in LA was broken into, her car vandalized." She held up another finger. "After she moved to Seattle, she had another break-in and was mugged and got a knife wound as a result."

"That should be in your database, Detective, along with the police report of the break-in." Lacey's voice was calm and cool. Clearly, this guy hadn't left a good impression on an earlier visit.

"Finally, you have the car accident, which was a result of someone running her off the road and a kidnapping." Celie finished with a huff. "Now do you see why she has security?"

"And who are you? A relative?" The detective gave Celie the once over and Kyle grinned at Saint's response. The big man stepped up, his dark face a mask of resolve.

"We're friends, as well as relatives of Ms. Burke's son. Has anyone found any evidence of his whereabouts?"

Branson shook his head, bent over his notes. "Why do you think the car was forced off the road?"

Lacey shifted, her face narrowing in pain. "I was in the middle lane of the road and the car came up behind me, bumped my rear end, and then, when I tried to move over into the right lane, followed me and advanced until it hit the back of the driver's side. I barely missed a couple of cars and then swerved off the road. I think I blacked out for a minute because when I opened my eyes, the airbag had deployed and a man was walking up to the car. I asked for help and that's when he pulled out the pistol."

"Why would anyone shoot you, Ms. Burke? Are you estranged from the boy's father? And why was there no child protective seat in the back? If you had a child in the car, you should have had a legal seat there as well."

She stared at the police officer. "I had a child seat in the car. Davey was strapped in. I remember looking back there and seeing him leaning a little to the side, as if the seat had tilted some but he was there. Why are you asking that question?"

"Because there wasn't a seat in the car when the police inspected it. And I went to the impound lot earlier. There's no seat there, Ms. Burke."

She didn't speak, just looked at the man as if he'd grown a couple more eyes in the minutes he'd been in the room. Kyle wondered, was she telling the truth about the kid? Or was she leading all of them on a wild goose chase? And why did he feel guilty for thinking those thoughts?

LACEY DREW IN A SHAKY BREATH. Her son, her life, was out of control. "I'm not lying to you, Detective.

Ask the other drivers. Someone had to see the accident, it was a busy street during rush hour. And you can check. I have a son. His name is David Anthony Burke." Lacey heard Celie make a comment but she didn't take it in, intent on making the police officer see reason.

"Where do you live, Ms. Burke. And work." The police officer questioned.

Lacey told him, sure he was only affirming information he'd already gained. "My boss lets me keep Davey with me at my job. Check with her. It's the Pinnacle Theater, downtown. I'm the wardrobe mistress."

"I'll give her a call." Detective Branson murmured then he glanced up at her. "Why would someone want to take your son, Ms. Burke?"

"I don't know!" She heard the wail in her voice but couldn't stop it. "I don't know why any of this is happening to me."

He asked several more questions, all dealing with the same issue. Why was her son taken? What had she done to endanger him? Who had a vendetta against her? Why had she left LA? Why move to Seattle, with no family or friends here? The questions started floating over her head, as if in speech bubbles and she ran a hand across her eyes in desperation, trying to come up with something, anything that would give him a pathway to finding her son. Finally, Kyle strode to the detective. "Look, she's exhausted. Can we do this another time? She doesn't have any more answers."

Detective Branson nodded and left a minute later, leaving the room in silence. Lacey shut her eyes against the hot tears threatening to overflow. If she let them start, she'd never stop crying.

"We're going downstairs to get something to eat," Saint said quietly. "Want anything?"

Lacey shook her head, sick at the thought. Kyle likewise declined the offer and the two left the room, closing the door behind them.

"Can you tell me the whole thing over again, Lacey? I just want to hear it from you, without the cop interfering."

She sighed and opened her eyes to take in the man seated beside her bed. He was big, but not overpowering. When she looked closer, she could tell he kept himself fit and in shape, but he didn't have muscles on top of muscles. His eyes, a cross between blue and gray, focused on her to the point she felt as if she were the only thing he was thinking about at this moment. He must be hell on wheels with other women, she mused, then was shocked she could even think of attraction and sex right now.

"Where do you want me to start?" She asked quietly.

"Are you too tired to do this?" he responded.

"No. I'm tired, yes but I want to figure this out."

She shifted her left arm into another, less achy position. Her shoulder, which she'd been told had been dislocated and reset, ached to the point she couldn't find a comfortable position.

"How about starting when you can remember feeling like something wasn't right."

She stared out into space and thought. "I guess it was around the time Davey was about sixteen months old. I'd been working out of town for a couple of weeks and I'd had some trouble finding short-term daycare in Canada." At his quizzical look, she continued. "I worked on wardrobe and costumes for films. Most of my work was done in LA but occasionally I'd get called to come on set for something, a change in costume, repairs, that sort of thing. I didn't have to go out of town often and I always took Davey when I did. Anyway, the site was this tiny town in Canada and they didn't have any daycare centers to speak of. I ended up having to take him with me on the job." She grinned at the memory of her small son, running behind the "monsters" during breaks and being chased by the same. "He loved it and the cast and crew were pretty good with him. There was just one guy that seemed to be put out by having him there."

"Who was that?" he asked.

"An assistant prop manager. He complained that Davey might get underfoot, even though I kept him in the wardrobe trailer and with me all the time.

The director overheard the props guy yelling at me about Davey and gave him a warning. I wasn't there long enough to get any more static from him."

Kyle asked for the man's name and filed it away to check on later. "Was that what made you uncomfortable?"

She shrugged. "I don't remember. I just recall feeling uneasy. It probably was him, though. I'd never had any issues with my work or my presence on set. I found my apartment broken into when I got home to LA." She grimaced. "I'd read accounts where people feel violated when their stuff is taken but I'd never experienced it. The police said it was probably just kids looking for drug money but it didn't feel that way." She frowned, "The TV was gone and a few pieces of jewelry, but mainly it was just trashed like someone was looking for something."

Kyle's radar went off at that statement. "You have no idea what they might have been looking for? And was your car broken into soon after that?"

She nodded, turning sharp eyes to him. "Yes. You think they're looking for something, don't you?"

He nodded. "I could be wrong but it sounds like it. You had that feeling with the apartment and the car. And honestly, if someone wanted you dead, not scared, you wouldn't be here now. You've lived through several attempts on your life and survived, including a close-range shot. Haven't you wondered at that?"

Lacey touched her side where the bullet had grazed a rib and hit soft tissue. The doctor had mentioned she was lucky in that the bullet missed all her major organs, including her liver. At the time, in her drug-induced haze, she'd been grateful but her attention had been on Davey since the accident. Now, she began to piece things together. "I hadn't thought of that. The guy was less than five feet away from me. He could have killed me easily, couldn't he?" When Kyle just stared at her, she took a shaky breath. "Then he just wanted to disable me so he could get to Davey."

"And probably to scare you even more than before." Kyle leaned forward and rested his elbows on his knees. "Look, Lacey, we need to figure out what information they think you have. If you do have it—" At her involuntary protest he held a hand up and continued, "If you have it and are not aware of its significance, we need to use it to get your son back."

"And if I don't have it?"

"We need to figure out what they're looking for and convince them you do. Otherwise, Davey will be in more danger than ever."

CHAPTER 3

THE DOCTOR DETERMINED that Lacey could be released that evening, given her progress. Since Kyle had arrived, she'd been up and walking several times, as well as refused any pain medication other than a mild over the counter tablet. Obviously, the doctor said, she was able to deal with the stitches and discomfort. She left the hospital with her entourage, as well as an order to return for a checkup in a week.

When they arrived at her apartment, Lacey teared up immediately upon entering. It smelled of her son. Though she knew the aromas of his favorite drink of grape juice, his bubble bath and berry flavored toothpaste couldn't be lingering, the place still released the scents from the very walls. Lacey took a steadying breath and entered, ushering everyone inside.

"I've not got a guest room, but I do have a pull-out sofa."

Celie shook off her concerns and smiled at Saint who returned the gesture with a chuckle. "When Celie and I first met we stayed in a few questionable places."

Lacey arched a brow and Celie laughed outright, her face glowing as she eyed her partner. "Saint was assigned to protect me. It's a story that takes a little time."

Lacey sighed, "Since I don't plan on sleeping any time soon, it sounds like a nighttime story."

While the others chatted, Kyle made a circuit through the apartment and disappeared into the kitchen, then the bedrooms. Lacey didn't hear any footfalls or items being moved but was reassured by the knowledge of his presence.

When he returned from Davey's room, his face was grim. In his hand he held a folded paper, the edge clasped between two fingertips. "I found this on Davey's bed."

Saint held his hand out for it but Lacey stopped him with a question. "Shouldn't we call the police? Detective Branson?"

"Let's see what it says first," Celie said, starting toward the kitchen. "Kyle, bring the note in here. We need to preserve any evidence that's on it. Lacey, do you have plastic wrap?"

Lacey found the roll and pulled off a sheet of

wrap then lay it on the counter. After Kyle placed it on the sheet, Celie took a butter knife and spoon and opened the note, carefully spreading the paper.

It was a single sheet of copy paper with computer-printed letters in bold. "Info for the kid." A phone number followed.

Lacey put her hand to her forehead. "What information? I don't know anything."

Celie touched her shoulder then gestured to the cabinets. "Do you have any coffee? I have a feeling we might need it."

While Celie bustled around finding coffee and cups, Lacey stared at the note. "I don't have any information. Why are they doing this?"

Kyle and Saint exchanged glances then Saint carefully covered the still opened note with another piece of plastic wrap, taking care to only touch the edges of the wrap itself. "We need to sit down and go through this."

"We'd started earlier," Kyle said as he led Lacey to the small kitchen table tucked into the corner of the room. A placemat made from a large piece of construction paper and covered with plastic held the place of honor in the center of the table. A child's scrawled drawing of what looked like a sun and two round faces decorated the piece. Lacey ran a finger over the image of the smaller circle then covered her face with her hands. "I don't know what to do. Do I call the police?"

"Not yet. We need to figure out what they want, whoever 'they' are." Kyle sat beside her and put his hand on her arm, gently pulling it down and uncovering her face. "We'll figure it out."

She breathed in, wanting to agree with him but having no idea where to start figuring the problem out. When she said as much, Saint sat on the other side of her. Celie, bringing two cups of coffee, served Lacey and Kyle then returned for two more. Lacey, used to lightened coffee, sipped the black brew and decided it was exactly what she needed right now.

An instant's silence was followed by Celie heading to the living room. She returned with a notebook and a laptop, which she handed to Saint. "This is how Luc and I work. We're going to figure out this thing. Let's start with the break-ins and go from there."

Lacey repeated her story for the innumerable time and then continued with her move to Seattle. "I hated LA after the break-ins. If there were kids in the neighborhood that wanted my stuff, I didn't want to know them. If there was something else going on, I wanted to get Davey away as soon as I could. I had a coworker who'd moved from LA to Seattle the year before. We'd kept in touch and she'd let me know about the Pinnacle looking for a replacement wardrobe mistress. The money was as good as what I'd made in LA and I jumped at the chance. This apartment is a sublet and I got a good deal on it as well. Everything seemed to fall into place." She sighed, "Until I got mugged a month ago."

"How long have you been in Seattle?" Celie asked, her head bent over her notebook and her pen scribbling. Lacey saw Celie was making a chart of some sort. Saint likewise was tapping away at his laptop. Kyle just sat and sipped at his coffee, his eyes intent on her. She felt the gaze through her, warming her frozen bones and blood. A sliver of hope, faint though it was, bloomed in her.

"About seven months. Davey was settling in well, he's a happy little boy. The theater manager lets me take him to work with me as long as we aren't in production or dress rehearsal. And even then, a daughter of one of the crew baby sits in the wardrobe room." She ran a finger over the rim of her cup. "I don't take chances with my son."

Kyle leaned back in his chair. "So, other than the props guy on the shoot, you haven't had any problem with others on the job?" She shook her head and, when asked, Kyle filled Celie and Saint in on the assistant props manager's complaints. Saint quickly tapped out some keys and within a minute had the man's location and had eliminated him as a likely candidate as Lacey's tormentor. "At least preliminarily. We'll keep him on the list, just in case." Saint said and looked up at Lacey. "Let's talk about your past. Any problems in high school? College? Any weird or crazy boyfriends? Girlfriends?"

Lacey smiled faintly. "I had an average high school career. I was involved in drama and a historical reenactment club in Boise where I grew up. I was a drama geek and a history nut. I "fell in love" with the guy that had the best fake British accent in the club and that lasted all of three months before he dumped me for the new girl with a larger bra size. When I went to college, I focused on theater and history, my two majors. I loved the costumes more than the stage so I dropped theater in my junior year, picked up a textiles minor. I got my degree and ended up in LA with several roommates for several years, trying to get a toe hold on the industry. By the time I met Tony I had made it to a decent sized film company and was making enough to have only one roommate."

Celie glanced up at the mention of her brother's name. "How did you and Tony meet?"

"At a party. I didn't do the club scene that much in LA, it was too expensive, to be honest. I agreed to go to a party for a coworker who was getting married. She was marrying a guy in the Army and said the whole thing would be different than the usual LA parties." Lacey smiled at the memory. "It was. We went to an old bar near the base and had burgers and beer and played pinball on old machines. That's where I met Tony. We competed at an Iron Maiden machine."

Celie chuckled. "He loved pinball. Said electronic games didn't take the finesse the old machines needed."

"He was good, very good. We played all evening and he made me laugh." Lacey looked down at her hands and smiled. "He came home with me that evening and stayed the weekend."

"Did you talk a lot?" Celie's question was odd, Lacey thought, and a little off-kilter, considering the thoughts she had of Tony. He'd been a passionate and fun lover, and one she wouldn't soon forget. But talking? They really hadn't much.

"Not that weekend. We texted quite a bit over the next few weeks. We didn't see each other over a couple of times after that. Either he was on duty or I was too busy. And then I found out I was pregnant."

Kyle, who'd been quiet and still, stood and went to refill his coffee. He stood with his back to the trio when he asked, "Was this guy supportive of you when you told him you were having a baby?"

Surprised at the flat tone of the question, Lacey nodded, though Kyle wouldn't be able to see her, "Sure. As I mentioned to Celie, he wanted to get married. It was me who was reluctant to go farther. I felt like we didn't know each other enough to make such a commitment. He'd still be able to be in the baby's life and if things worked out, then we'd go from there."

"So where is this guy?" Kyle turned and stared at her, his gaze intent.

"He's dead, Kyle." Saint inserted quietly then turned to look at the man still guarding the coffee pot. "That's right, you don't know the history. Celie is Tony's sister. And Lacey had her name as an emergency contact so when she was hurt, we were contacted."

"So, you guys knew each other," Kyle advanced and stood beside Lacey.

"No. And I wondered, why did you have my name in your ICE information?" Celie asked, her gaze purposefully avoiding Kyles.

"I was planning on contacting you and asking you to help. At least to take care of Davey. I was afraid he'd get hurt or worse, what with the things that were happening to me." She shuddered. "And he has. Oh, God."

They had to take a break then. The control she'd been hanging onto for the last few days crumbled and Lacey started crying, then found she couldn't stop. Kyle and Saint stood still as statues as Celie led her into her bedroom and, after a brief argument, convinced her to take an over the counter sleep aid. As she drifted off, Lacey heard murmurs in the other room and hoped against hope the three ex soldiers would come up with a miracle that would save her son.

CHAPTER 4

Kyle heaved a breath and, taking care not to look toward Lacey's bedroom, headed to the living room. It was the farthest place from her bedroom and they might be able to make some sense of all of this. He plopped down in an easy chair, leaving the sofa to the others. "What the hell is going on here?"

Saint shook his head and held his arm out for Celie. She tucked her body under his arm and leaned into him. The couple sat together, their bodies blending in as if they couldn't bear to be apart. Kyle had never felt that before with any human being. What must it be like? His senses broadened to take in the apartment, to absorb what Lacey Burke must be like.

A bookcase held books that looked like a blend of fiction, reference, and kid's books. One photo graced the top of the piece of furniture, a candid photo enlarged to fit in a small frame, a woman holding a bundle.

Other than a television, too small to effectively watch a ballgame, the matched neutral furniture, and several framed pictures of women dressed in long, elaborate gowns, the living room was minimalist, compared to those of other women he'd "dated". Was she the same? All about her job and her son? Or was she hiding something?

"I think she's telling us all she knows," Celie answered his question in a neutral tone and Kyle glanced around at her to find her eyeing him with suspicion. "You think she's hiding something, don't you?" she continued.

"I think there's more to this situation than we've found, obviously. And how do you know she's being upfront with us? You haven't known her any longer than I have."

Celie shrugged, "Intuition. I think if she did know anything she'd spill it. Her son is at risk. And I saw her when she finally agreed to take that pill. She was on the verge of breaking down but didn't want to lose her control. She's not someone who would lie to protect herself at the risk of her child."

Saint intervened before Kyle could respond. "Okay, let's say she's given us all she knows, consciously. There could be something she's not aware she knows." He leaned away with a grimace and rubbed his side. "I didn't say she is lying C, I just said she might not be aware of anything."

"Fine." Celie stood and walked to the photo that Kyle had seen before. Taking it off the shelf, she studied it for a minute and then turned around, her eyes filled. "Tony had a son."

Kyle turned away when Saint stood and went to the woman, enfolding her in his arms. Though he appreciated the sentiment, they needed to get back on the subject.

"How did Tony get killed, anyway?" When Saint threw him a glare over Celie's shoulder, Kyle shrugged. "It might have some bearing."

Saint waggled his head. "Doubt it. Tony found some evidence of drug smuggling and got killed for it. I doubt he shared any of that information with Lacey. From what we know about the situation, he wasn't too far into looking into the problem when he was killed."

"But what if he casually said something or texted something to Lacey?" Celie shrugged out of Saint's embrace, the picture clasped in her hand. "It's a possibility."

"And the guy that's been threatening Lacey thinks he's going to get a windfall of info when he's going to get sweet nothings that Tony sent?" Kyle bit out, his mind going to what could have been in the texts and emails.

"Maybe." Celie frowned at him. "At least it's a lead we didn't have before."

"So, when she wakes up we'll ask Lacey if we can eavesdrop on her lover's texts," he muttered and slouched into the chair's confines.

They discussed other options, including going through a storage unit, if Lacey had one. Rifling through family papers, assuming Lacey kept records of stuff like that. And what was her family history? Was there anything of significance in that?

All in all, they came up with possibilities that they hadn't had before but no real leads, from Kyle's point of view. They all turned in, the couple on the pull-out sofa with a spare blanket Celie rounded up and Kyle on the hallway floor hall with another blanket wrapped around him. Kyle's mood was as dark as it could be off the battlefield. And damn if he didn't dream of sexting with Lacey.

Around dawn, Lacey stumbled from her room, muzzy with the sleep aid and sore all over. Her shoulder ached, her side pulled from the stitches and she was sure she'd not left a bundle of laundry in the hall, between her and the much-needed bathroom. When the bundle moved, she shrieked, bringing the whole house awake.

"Damn it! I need to go to the bathroom," she muttered and stepped around the now seated man in the dark pants and shirt. Without his face shining in the predawn light, she would have stepped on top of him, he was that still.

But she heard his chuckle behind her as she made her way to the toilet and slammed the door. After a few minutes of splashing water and a brush through her hair, Lacey exited the room, only to find Celie waiting impatiently. "I started the coffee," she said and then darted into the bathroom.

Lacey returned to her bedroom, this time without obstacles, and dressed. As she did, her mind cleared and the weight of the situation bore down on her. Her son was with someone he didn't know, someone who could harm him. And she'd been unaware of it for hours.

She made it to the kitchen and the coffee pot before she made eye contact with Kyle and Saint. Both were standing at the opened refrigerator and staring into it. Lacey ignored them and poured the coffee then went to the living room where her favorite photo of her and Davey sat. She stared at it, promising her son, no matter what, she'd find him.

"We have some ideas," Kyle's soft voice behind her sent a surge of unwelcome warmth through her and she turned.

"What kind of ideas?"

He ushered her back into the kitchen where they found Saint at the stove, browning sausage with eggs and bread alongside. Kyle pushed her into a chair and then retrieved his own coffee. "We have a few things we can talk about, look into, to see if they have anything to do with what this guy is looking for."

"So, you don't have a plan to save Davey."

"Didn't say that," Saint responded. "We need to know what this guy is looking for before we call him. And we need to do that today." He pushed the toaster lever down on two slices of bread and then cracked eggs into the pan.

"And if we don't have the information?"

"We lie," Kyle said and stood to help with breakfast.

THEY ATE their meal while going over the things they'd come up with. Lacey had no storage unit so that was a bust. When asked about her family, she was short and to the point. Her parents had divorced when she was young and her father left the region. He'd had another family and died when she was in college. "I've never really connected with his other family. My mom wasn't okay with it and they didn't seem too enthusiastic at the funeral either. Anyway, I haven't had any contact with them either before or after the funeral." She fiddled with her fork before tossing it down on the half-eaten food. "My mom died two years ago, right after Davey was born, from breast cancer."

Kyle noticed she'd played with her food more than eaten it but didn't say anything. She'd gotten enough to keep going and God knows, he knew how little it took to keep a person alive for a few days. And he'd find the kid, he had to.

"And the texts? The emails from Tony?" He asked, dreading her answer. She shrugged and retrieved her cell phone from her bedroom. She swiped and tapped a few times and then held it out to him. "We didn't talk about a lot. His job, my job. He couldn't believe I got paid for making costumes and I had no clue what he did, really." She sighed, running a hand through her long blonde hair. "The emails were more of the same. People trying to get to know each other when we couldn't see each other in person."

Celie picked up the dishes and took them to the sink. Lacey started to stand to wash and got waved off. "Let's retrieve those emails. Do you have a printer?" Celie headed off, presumably for the ever-present notebook and laptop, and Lacey went in another room, Kyle and Saint following.

In half an hour, all of the texts and emails were printed off, via Saint's computer skills. The quartet sat around the table and began to read the messages and passed them around, making low comments. Kyle didn't acknowledge his relief as he read the texts and messages. There were a few mentions of kisses and so on but nothing blatant. Still, there was enough to raise the beast in him.

"Here's something," Celie held up a hand and read, 'I've never been disappointed in my fellow servicemen but I wonder about this one guy. He's not in my unit, but he's constantly around. I've noticed him lurking around the pallets and there's no reason for it.'" Celie looked up at Saint. "I wonder if that was Evans."

"No mention of his name?" Saint held out his hand and she handed him the sheet.

"Nope."

"Do you remember this thread, Lacey?" Celie motioned and Saint passed the paper to Lacey who read over it. She nodded, "He was uneasy. He'd been less friendly in his texts and less frequent too. I remember thinking the romance was probably fizzling, with the distance and not seeing each other. And it was right before I found out I was pregnant."

"He was probably preoccupied with the evidence he was finding," Celie said and picked up another sheet. This time her face stilled. "Did anyone check out the attachment on this email?"

No one responded and she sighed, then gestured to Saint and the laptop, giving the date for the email. When he pulled up the item in question, Lacey leaned forward for a closer look. A photo, a selfie of Tony took up a portion of the screen. "It was a picture he sent me when we were talking about where we worked. I couldn't get an idea of the scope of the place."

"He'd have worked in an office environment as well as going to the warehouses. He'd made corporal by the time he died, so he'd have had more office duties than warehouse ones," Celie murmured as she studied the photo. "Can you enlarge that, Luc?"

After he'd enlarged the photo all four of them studied the picture. Tony, smiling, must have held the phone even with his face, as that was all that was visible of him. Behind him, a couple of men talked near stacks and pallets of goods, sealed, ready to ship out or to be inventoried. Kyle studied the faces of the men behind Tony. "Do you have any photo enhancement skills, Saint?"

"A few," Saint replied and started to work. "Give me a few minutes."

Kyle stood and went to the coffee maker where he started a fresh pot. Celie and Lacey worked on the dishes and within a short time, all were back at the table, anxious. Saint finished the enhancement and then, with a few muttered words, tapped out some more commands. He cursed and looked up at the group. "I have a feeling we've found the info."

"What?" Lacey asked, her voice faint. Kyle stepped up beside her in a silent show of support.

Saint turned the laptop around for the others to

see. Two photos were displayed. The first photo was of a young man and one older, both smiling and very well dressed. They were obviously related, as the older man looked like a mature version of the one at his side. The second photo, a cropped version of Tony's selfie, featured the same young man in a nice suit, alongside another, uniformed man. The suited man was handing the soldier something. "It's Evans," Celie blurted.

"Yeah, but that's probably not the focus here, especially since he's dead and buried." Saint pointed to one picture and then the other. "This is Grayson Mitchell, Jr. The only son and heir of Senator Grayson Mitchell. Member of the Armed Services Committee and an outspoken supporter of the military. The fact that this guy," Saint pointed to the picture of Junior and Evans, "was mixed up with Troy may just be what the kidnapper is looking for."

"Why? What significance does that have?" Lacey looked thoroughly confused and Kyle lost any doubt he'd had that she was holding back information.

"Troy Evans was heavily involved in a drug distribution ring Saint and I uncovered a few months ago. It's huge. Tony found some discrepancies in shipments to overseas units. Those shipments had drugs added to them and Troy was responsible for getting them into the overseas shipments. When Tony started looking into the matter, he was killed." Celie looked at Lacey, her expression set. "We've found the link between the kidnapping and you. It was Tony and this picture."

"Maybe more information is somehow embedded in his communication," Saint muttered.

Lacey shook her head but Celie gestured toward the picture. "Just like the weight discrepancy. Tony probably didn't think it was a big deal either and he ended up dead. This is a huge organization, Lacey, and one we can't deal with on our own. We need to contact the DEA."

"First we need to call the kidnappers. I want my son back." Lacey insisted and Kyle agreed.

"They won't wait for long," he said, taking in all of the others. "We can't either."

CHAPTER 5

DESPITE HIS MISGIVINGS, Kyle allowed Celie and Saint to make a call to a DEA agent they'd worked with. Agent Simpson was in Kansas City and not available to meet with them online until later in the day so Kyle insisted on making a call to the kidnapper. "We need to at least let him know we're taking him seriously."

"And the police?" Lacey asked as she stood to go to the counter where the note still lay.

"Later. If the DEA wants to involve the cops here, that's up to them. I'd just as soon have fewer officials in this mess as possible."

They sat around the table, a notepad on the little placemat and a pen resting beside it. The plan was that Lacey make the call and put it on speaker. Any other communication would have to be silent, written.

She dialed the number and waited. When the speaker came online, it was distorted, put through a voice changing software. "Do you have it?"

Lacey glanced at the list of questions they wanted answered. "Where is my son?"

That hadn't been on the list but then it didn't need to be either.

"The kid is fine."

"I want to talk to him." She sounded sure of herself, not the mess she'd been the night before, and Kyle's respect inched higher. She needed to be strong, strong enough to battle this man who had her son.

"When I get the info."

"What info are you looking for?" She asked.

"Don't fuck with me, bitch. I want the picture and the list."

Kyle glanced up at Lacey who shook her head. Celie and Saint in turn shrugged.

"I want proof you haven't hurt my son. If he is unharmed, I'll give you the photo. If you can't prove he's okay, it's going to the police."

Saint held up a hand and shook his head. Celie also gestured with a hand mimicking a tamping down motion. Lacey ignored them both. "I have what you want but you won't see it unless I get proof my son is well." She disconnected the line and pushed away from the table. With a whimper, she stood and fled down the hall.

Kyle followed her until he faced a closed bathroom door. Beyond, he could hear the retching sounds. He opened the door and found a washcloth then wet it. Handing it to her, he leaned against the sink and watched as she sat on the bathtub rim and bathed her face. Then she stood and nudged him out of the way, turning on water and splashing her face then rinsing her mouth.

She stood and faced him then, her lashes wet from water or tears, and said, "Did I just kill my own son?"

Kyle didn't know what to say. She'd taken a risk none of them had anticipated, one he figured she hadn't planned as well. Would it pan out? Or was she right, had she sealed her son's fate?

He did the only thing he knew to do in that minute. "Hell, no. You called his bluff. He wants that photo. He'll pay the price, it's not a big one."

He wrapped an arm around her awkwardly and squeezed her shoulders then stepped away. The man who could flirt his way into any woman's pants was acting like a middle school kid. When had that happened?

They went into the kitchen where Saint was busy at the computer. He'd tried to triangulate the phone call and had been partially successful. "He's in the state, not in the Seattle area. We need a map, a printed one. You guys think you can go out and pick one up?" He looked at Kyle and Lacey. Kyle bit back a curse.

Clearly, Saint and Celie thought it was a good idea to distract Lacey. "We won't be going anywhere. We can monitor the computer and phone while you two run the errand." His look must have filled in the blanks because Saint and Celie soon had their jackets on and were out the door with orders to pick up at least three burn phones in addition to the map.

"Why did they need a map? And why aren't we going to get one?" Lacey said, her face still pale and wan.

"To triangulate and plan. It's sometimes easier to do it with hard copies of maps rather than digital. And we didn't go because you have a sore shoulder, a gunshot wound, and are still a target. If you were out of the picture, the photo would be moot, since it's in your email."

She nodded dully then went to the refrigerator and removed a soft drink. Holding it up, she offered him one. When he saw it was diet he shook his head.

When she wandered into the living room, he plucked up the phones and laptop and followed her. Once he'd arrayed all of the electronics on the coffee table in front of them, he flicked on the small television and started roaming channels. Beside him, Lacey sipped at the soft drink and stared at the computer screen.

Once he'd found something he thought she'd watch and he could tolerate, a show about buying vacation homes, he reached out and tilted the laptop screen so it wasn't readily visible. "Do you ever think about leaving Seattle for someplace warmer?"

The television displayed a tropical paradise setting with beach frolickers and white sands. She glanced over at him then murmured. "Never to live. The magic would fade too quickly."

"How so?" He'd slouched into the curve of the sofa and swiveled his head toward her, only to find that she'd done the same thing, her eyes on the television and her spine curled into the couch.

"When you reserve a place for special times like holidays or vacations, it has a glow that your memories enhance. Everyday chores like maneuvering traffic in rush hour, buying foods that have to be imported onto an island, trash day, none of them are important. On vacation, you're willing to stop and let whole families cross in front of you. If you lived in that place, your daily commute would be interrupted by tourists. You'd have to plan outings around holidays and peak times. I think it'd take the shine off the experience."

He studied her. Her bruises were fading into green and yellow but couldn't lessen the classic lines beneath them. She might not be a beauty in the sense of today's fashions, but with her straight nose, light eyes, and pale complexion, she resembled a classic painting, a woman out of time. When she turned to look at him, to likewise study him, his breath stopped and he wondered how much trouble he'd get in if he leaned over and kissed her.

In that instant, a message pinged on a phone and both of them shot to a straight posture.

"It's mine," she breathed and swiped her phone then took a shaky breath. "Davey."

The picture was of a little boy with a tear-stained face and unruly hair. He was seated on a ratty looking couch with a newspaper beside him, today's paper. The New York Times.

"They've bought a Times. Smart, since we'd not be able to tell where they were, if we didn't track the message."

She didn't respond, just held the phone and studied her son's image. Kyle let her be, she needed the time. And her bet had paid off.

He noted the time the photo was sent and then stood and started planning. If they were going to give the guy the photo and ensure Davey's safety, they had to have some plan to lure the guy to them.

Possibilities ran through his mind. Meet up and exchange the boy for the phone? Might work. Send the photo via the internet and they'd never see Davey again. And what about the list? What list? He returned to the couch and opened the laptop, then realized it was password protected.

"Can we take a look at your texts, Lacey? We need to see if Tony sent you a list."

"He didn't, at least in an attachment," her breath was a whisper and her eyes were still fixed on the photo.

"Did he send you any more photos?"

She looked at him, her frustration evident at his interruption but then nodded. "A couple or three, I think. After he quit contacting me I decided I needed to ignore the texts." She smiled, her face wry. "I couldn't bring myself to delete the texts, though. I guess I wanted them to remember him by."

Kyle asked the question that had been bugging him ever since he'd learned of Tony Garcia. "You still hung up on him?"

She looked surprised, "No. I'm not even sure I was in love with him, to begin with. He was great, don't get me wrong. But we'd not really had a lot of time together and texting, emailing, that sort of thing, to me doesn't tell you a lot about a person."

"So, a fling?"

"A fling that gave me a wonderful gift," she glanced back at the photo she kept refreshing.

Kyle nodded then motioned to the phone. "You want to wait til Saint and Celie get back to look at the photos?"

She sighed and shook her head. "No. We need to find that list, if it exists." She closed the photo and found the other pictures Tony had sent her. With a few swipes and taps, they'd sent the photos to the printer, enlarged as much as possible. She also sent them to Saint's email, which would have to wait for the others.

Kyle eyed the grainy images. A desk was in the background of two of the three pictures but nothing was clear enough to read. "Saint will have to try to enhance these as well," he said and then stood and stretched.

The energy he tried to tamp down all the time had been absent over the past few hours. Now, he could feel it rising in him, a force swelling within seeking an outlet. If he could run, work out, it'd tamp it down. Instead, he was here, with a woman he found too appealing, too vulnerable, and off limits because of that.

"Are you okay?" She turned to watch him as he strode around the tiny room.

"Just restless."

"I guess you aren't used to being sedentary." She gestured to a small cabinet tucked into the corner of the room. "I'm used to sitting at the sewing machine or drafting board for hours. Or reading. With Davey, exercise isn't a problem either."

He shrugged. When on a mission, he could lie motionless for hours if needed but his senses would be on high alert. Now, he had energy to spare and nowhere to expend it. Her apartment, an inner one, had few spots vulnerable to intruders, other than the doors and a couple of windows. He had too much idle time on his hands.

"Do you need to go running or something? I'm sure I'll be fine here, alone."

He scoffed. "No way." He glanced toward the hall. It might be a place he could do some pushups or sit-ups, though he knew they wouldn't take the edge off.

The key jangled in the door at that moment and he was in front of Lacey, his hand cradling his pistol. When Celie entered the room, a couple of plastic bags slung over her arm, he relaxed slightly, then more so when Saint followed and closed then locked the door.

"Any developments?"

Kyle filled Saint in and then, with a sigh of relief, went outside to 'reconnoiter'.

He reconnoitered for half an hour, at a fast clip. He'd ran almost five miles, according to his phone, before he felt calm enough to return to the apartment. When he knocked on the door, Saint answered, a question on his face. "Just looking around. Nothing up."

"Good, looks like you got some monkeys off your back, too." Saint grinned slightly and Kyle tilted his head in acknowledgment. Ex soldiers recognized the feeling.

They discussed the options in delivering the photo. Saint sent a copy to Hank Patterson, the head of Brotherhood Protectors, with a question about contacting the DEA. "That way, we have some backup."

"And if they find out we've distributed the photo?" Lacey's tone was querulous. Saint hadn't asked her opinion first, after all.

"I asked him to hold on to it til we make the transfer," Saint reassured her.

"We need to find the list," Kyle reminded them and then told them of his and Lacey's attempts to read the photos they'd found. Saint went to work on his end and Celie joined Lacey to study Davey's picture. "He looks like Tony," Celie murmured and Lacey smiled. "He really does. His hair is so curly, though."

"Tony's was too. He had to keep it buzzed cut in the Army or he said he got ribbed about it." Celie ran a hand over the curly ponytail she sported. "Our whole family has bushy hair."

Kyle looked away, his mind on the man who'd captured Lacey's attention, even for a brief time. Had Tony Garcia not been killed, would they have ended up together? Married? And how in the hell could he be jealous of a dead man?

CHAPTER 6

THE PHONE PINGED and Lacey jumped to read the text. "You got picture. Where's mine?"

"What do we do?" Lacey glanced around at them all.

"We set up a physical drop. Otherwise, we'll not know where or how long he'll keep Davey." Or if he'll give him back, Kyle thought. Two year olds weren't deemed trustworthy when testifying but who knew whether this guy was sane or calm enough to trust that?

Lacey nodded and looked at Saint. "Do I respond now? Wait?"

"Now. We need to decide what to tell him, though." Saint studied the folded maps and then started unfolding one with Celie taking his lead and unfolding another. "Damn. I wish we had a way of tracking him."

"We can after we send the picture," Celie murmured and Saint suddenly lunged over the kitchen table and kissed her soundly. "Yes, we can, darlin. And that's all the more reason to send the bastard the photo." He turned to Lacey and started talking.

Fifteen minutes later, Lacey sat before the group, her cell phone in front of her. She dialed the number from the last incoming call. Two rings later, a distorted voice came over the speaker. "You haven't sent the picture and the list. You sure you want to see your son?"

"I do, I do. I just don't have the list ready yet."

"What's to get ready? It's a fucking list." The panic and anger came through crystal clear as the four listened and Kyle scribbled a note for Lacey.

"It was on several photos. I haven't found all of them on my phone yet," Lacey raised an eyebrow at the blatant lie but Kyle was shooting for extra time at this point. Who knew where the damn list was or if Lacey even had it.

"I can send you the photo, as a show of my good faith."

"Good faith? You call the cops? That's cop talk."

"No! No, I just guess I've heard it on a TV show or something. I swear I haven't called the police. On my son's life, I haven't." She grimaced when she said the latter and Kyle had the feeling she was bleeding inside.

"Send it. We'll see." Then the call was disconnected. Kyle turned to watch Saint as he planted a code in the photo file and then sent it from his computer to Lacey's phone. She in turn sent it to the kidnapper.

"Now, we wait til he opens the file. Hopefully, he doesn't have the smarts to know we can trace him from the photo."

"And we look for the damned list." Celie sighed, running a hand over her ponytail.

They enlarged the photos and tried enhancing the area on the desk with no luck. Finally, Saint, who'd been at the computer with his attention divided between the uploaded photo and the enhancement process cursed and pushed away from the computer. "I need a drink."

Lacey shook her head, "I don't have any liquor in the house. I don't drink often enough to keep it."

He grinned and gestured toward Celie. "We took care of that when we went out earlier."

Kyle, worried that any break they took could result in disaster, stared Saint down. "We need to keep working."

"Who said I couldn't drink and work at the same time?" Saint threw over his shoulder as he walked over to the backpack and extracted a couple of bottles. One was wine and the other a flavored liqueur. Kyle sputtered a laugh as he watched the big African American pour a small amount of what looked like chocolate-flavored liqueur into four glasses. Saint passed them around and ended with putting one in front of Kyle with a glare. "This gets out to the Brotherhood and your ass is grass, man."

Kyle toasted the man with his drink and sipped it. It tasted like a dessert ought to taste. "Not a Bud but not bad." Kyle pushed the drink to the side and leaned onto the table, rubbing his forehead. "If the list isn't in the photos, we need to go through the emails and texts again."

Lacey sipped at her drink but Kyle could tell she wasn't a fan. "I don't think the list would be in text form. They were always short, no more than a couple of sentences at most."

"Could the list be over several texts?" Lacey said, her eyes on Saint as he tapped on the laptop, taking a break now and then to sip at his own drink.

"I suppose so but why? Why would Tony send me a list of anything that a drug dealer would want?" Lacey stood and took her drink to the sink and poured it down the drain, rinsing the glass afterward. Then she turned and faced the others. "I think this is a wild goose chase."

"What happens if we tell this guy, assuming it's Mitchell, that we don't have the list. Will he believe us?" Celie looked from one person to the other and Kyle knew the answer was in all of their expressions. No way would Mitchell believe they didn't have the list and Davey would pay the price.

"So, we need to figure out what the list was. A list of people in the organization? A list of units the shipments were going to? A list of dates?" Lacey said absently then looked up at Celie. "It had to be the units, the places the shipments were going to, didn't it? Wouldn't that be the logical thing Tony would be tracking?"

"Probably, but the dates would be important, too. We need to narrow down what would be most injurious to this guy, Mitchell. How it would figure into his involvement." Kyle said and then turned to Saint when he heard him grunt.

"We've got him." Saint looked up and grinned. "He opened the file. He's in a neighborhood just outside of the city."

"So we can move on him," Kyle smiled back at Saint and the old energy returned.

LACEY WATCHED as all three of them went into military mode. She'd known the former soldiers still trained and kept up to date on their weapons skills. The fact that all three worked for private security firms made up of ex-servicemen and specialists explained that. But now she saw the enthusiasm with which Saint, Celie, and especially Kyle went about planning what amounted to a raid. She hugged herself and said a prayer for all of them.

When Kyle turned to her and told her Celie

would be staying with her she sent the other woman a surprised look. Celie shrugged, resigned. "You're at risk, remember? Even if we're reasonably sure Mitchell is in this thing on his own, we don't want to take any chances." Celie finished tightening a strap along Saint's naked back and Lacey uttered a gasp when she realized the strap was attached to a prosthesis.

Saint grinned at her, "Didn't realize I'm part cyborg? That's why I wear the Michael glove." He raised his left hand which he kept covered with a black nylon glove. This he removed and replaced with one that looked like leather but more supple. "Thanks, by the way."

"For what?" Lacey breathed.

"For not noticing." He returned and pulled down his shirt then shrugged on a jacket.

Kyle had been at work while Lacey and the other two talked and now approached her, his head covered with a dark baseball cap, his eyes shadowed by the brim. He wore an earpiece, had a jacket on with a bulge at the side, and a dangerous look in his eye.

"We'll get Davey back safe and sound, I promise." He said and to her surprise, leaned down and kissed her. The contact was brief, too brief to be called affectionate, but still managed to both shock and arouse her. By the time she had breath to protest, if she was going to, he was out the door and Celie was smiling at her. "Happens all the time."

They waited and Lacey noticed Celie checking her phone frequently. Where were they?

"What are they planning?" Lacey asked.

"Just to find where Davey is being held and get him out. Contact the police afterward."

"With Mitchell being a senator's son, do you think it'll work? I mean, the senator has been in Washington for a long time." The Mitchell family was an old guard Washington fixture. Though the family hailed from the Midwest, they had held offices in Washington, either in Congress, as ambassadors or aides to presidents, for generations. For a Mitchell to be involved in a drug organization would send shockwaves through the capitol.

They spent the next few minutes tidying up from the ops prep, as well as rinsing the few glasses and putting away the alcohol. When a knock sounded at the door, Lacey didn't think twice and went to answer it. Before Celie could stop her she opened the door to a young man dressed in jeans and a t-shirt emblazoned with a local pizzeria. "Pizza." He said, and held out a box.

"We didn't order—"

A knife flashed and Lacey cried out, her hand blazing with fire. A blur of movement beside her and a shove knocked her to the floor and she instinctively curled into a ball, waiting for something to happen. A rescue or another slash of pain?

A curse followed the sound of running feet brought her head up and Lacey saw Celie sprinting down the hall with the boy ahead of her. A knife, stained with blood, lay on the floor in front of the door. Lacey gingerly picked it up, her fingers shaking, and noticed more blood dripping from her palm. Once she had the knife inside the doorway, she shut the door and leaned against the wall. She had to stand up and get something to staunch the blood on her palm, to see how bad the cut was. But where was Celie?

Her mind cleared and with a cry, Lacey pulled the door open and peered outside. Celie, her face thunderous, stalked down the hall, her hand wrapped around her side. "Get inside." She barked and Lacey retreated.

She retrieved a clean kitchen towel and wrapped her hand in it then turned to Celie, who had become pale and wore a pinched look. "Where were you hurt?"

"It's okay." Celie waved a hand at her but Lacey saw the blood on it and pushed Celie toward the sofa. "Sit down. Let me see. We might need to go to the emergency room."

"No. No doctors. We'd have to report it and we don't need to do that right now." Celie grimaced as she raised her shirt to reveal a red slice along her ribcage. "I need some butterflies, that's all. There's some in my backpack."

Lacey swore and found the pack lying near the sofa. "You guys are crazy. And why aren't we to call the police?"

"Because they'd want to be involved in the kidnapping case and you know what a mess that'll become. If the senator's son has any inkling the authorities are involved, he'll run and take Davey with him. Or worse. Now, do you have any alcohol? And your hand is dripping."

They took turns ministering to each other. Lacey's wound was a puncture and, with more pressure and antiseptic, soon just ached under the thick bandage Celie wrapped around it. Celie's wound, however, required a box of what she called butterfly bandages, as well as liquid bandage, which looked a lot like super glue to Lacey. When she asked Celie about the worry of a scar, Celie just laughed and said it'd be a badge of honor. "Nothing I haven't seen before." At Lacey's look of concern, Celie rushed to reassure her. "It's no more than what they'd do at a clinic. The liquid bandage will seal it and I shouldn't have more than a hairline scar, assuming I don't play around with it."

"Play around with what? And what the hell? Is that blood in the carpet?" Saint thundered. He and Kyle stood in the open doorway, their expressions mirror images of a mix of rage and terror.

"How did it go?" Celie asked, her face expressionless.

"It didn't," Kyle answered, his eyes sharp on Lacey. "What the hell happened here?"

"We had a little delivery," Celie answered and stood gingerly. Saint immediately started looking her over and then pulled her into the kitchen.

Kyle sat and studied Lacey. "What happened?"

"It was my fault. I thought it was you knocking at the door. I answered and it was a kid, had a pizza box. Then he pulled out a knife." She sighed and held up her hand. "I just got a poke in the hand, but Celie had a pretty nasty slash on her side."

"Damn it." He muttered and then reached for her hand. As he studied it, his head bent over it, Lacey couldn't help but study the little swirl of hair at his crown. He kept his hair shorn close to the scalp, making the little pattern all the more interesting.

"You aren't angry with me?"

"For answering the door without waiting for Celie to check it out? A little, but not enough to get out of shape about." He looked at her then, his face set in lines of determination. "You know what this means, don't you?"

She shook her head.

"Mitchell is still gunning for you, or someone he's hired. We need to get you someplace safe, tonight."

CHAPTER 7

THE CAR, a supercharged sedan, wasn't what Lacey had pictured Kyle driving. He looked more like a truck kinda guy, she mused as she watched him maneuver the Seattle traffic with ease. "I still don't understand why we had to split up."

"Mitchell and his associate know you had a woman with you. If they somehow identify Celie, they'll also figure Saint is close by. By splitting up, we at least have some element of the unknown with us."

She shook her head, "It shouldn't matter. And they'd be more of us to research."

He glanced at her, his expression lost in the gloom of the car. "We're going to have scheduled check-ins. And it's not like we'll be out of contact range, no matter where we are." He gestured to the cell phone tucked into the cup holder. "Nowadays, it's almost impossible to be isolated."

Unless it was emotional isolation, she mused and stared out the car window. What was Davey doing right now? Was he scared? Or had he adjusted to a new place without her? And what was she thinking! It was her son, her flesh and blood. She heaved a breath. "We have to figure out that blasted list."

He nodded. "Let's use the time now to try, then. You thought it might be dates or times? A list of weights?"

She shrugged, "I don't remember Tony sending anything like that. That's why I thought we might find the lists in the background of the photos."

He flicked a light on over her seat and she pulled the enlarged pictures. Before splitting up Celie had made copies of all of the texts, emails, and photos. Each couple would go through them searching for clues regarding a list. But in the artificial light, it was almost impossible to read anything in the background. Lacey tucked the photos back into the folder and rummaged to retrieve the other, thicker envelope of texts and emails. "I feel like we're spinning our wheels with all of this."

"We might be, but for now, that's all we have." He said and, upon hearing her sigh, placed his hand over hers as it lay on the sheaf of papers. "Saint is going to keep looking for a way to track Mitchell down. And he's also going to call his boss. There may be more on this Mitchell guy than we know about."

Lacey turned to him then and asked him to take the next exit. "Why?"

"There's a shopping center off the exit. I want a laptop." She muttered, regretting not bringing her own from her apartment.

Within half an hour they had a laptop, a car charger and were back on the road. She unpacked everything and had the device charging within minutes. "I know we can do searches with our phones, but I'd feel more comfortable with a computer right now. And with Saint's help, we might be able to get some research done on Mr. Mitchell. It's high time we find out who exactly we're dealing with."

Kyle found a motel room a mile off the main road and into the Cascades foothills. The room was tucked in against the scrub brush and a view of the road was the best part of the place. Lacey placed her backpack on the bed, along with the laptop, which she'd been cradling like a child. Kyle eyed her as she surveyed the room with its old fashioned television, desk phone, and alarm clock, all from the previous century. Thankfully, the place looked clean or he had the feeling they would have been back on the road searching for the next motel.

He could say one thing for her, she hadn't complained. Hadn't complained about discomfort from her sore shoulder or still smarting side wound, nor had she mentioned the fresh wound on her palm. He'd made sure they had bandages when they stopped and he'd be damned if she got any more war scars from this experience.

He tossed his small duffel onto the other side of the bed then stared at it. One bed. Had Lacey noticed? She'd disappeared into the bathroom upon their arrival. Now, she stood at vanity and stared into the mirror, her arms wrapped around herself. Kyle cursed his libido as he remembered her son.

He approached her and held out his hand. "Let's get the food out of the car and eat. Then we'll get to work." When she tucked her hand into his, he recognized the need. He needed to make this woman safe and reunite her with her son. And he needed to find a way to stay in her life. Somehow.

They ate the fast food meal they'd bought on the way to the motel. While the burgers were filling, they were far from satisfying and Kyle promised himself a decent meal after all of this was over. He glanced at his watch and dialed Saint's number to check in. "Hey, we're about two hours out of Seattle, near Ashford. I figured we'd get off the interstate."

"Good idea. Stay off the beaten path. We drove north. Ended up near Silverton. Celie is setting up the laptop. I'm going to give Hank a call after we talk. I'll let you know what he thinks."

"You think he'll want to call in the DEA?" Kyle watched as Lacey cleared the small desk area of drinks and started setting up the laptop.

"He was going to send the photo to them after we uploaded it to Mitchell, so they're already involved," Saint said. "The question is, will it come to anything. I haven't done nearly enough research on Mitchell to know if he has any priors or is a person of interest in any DEA files."

"And how much influence his father has," Kyle added.

"From what we read last night, he has a lot. He's been in Washington for decades and his family is entrenched in the city, as well. Hopefully, we can get past that."

Kyle heard the same doubt in Saint's voice as he experienced.

"We'll start with the texts and the emails. I'll get back to you in an hour."

When he disconnected, Kyle turned to Lacey, who was seated at the desk and watching him. "You think Mitchell will get away with it, don't you?"

"It's our job to make sure he doesn't," he returned and went to hunker down in front of her. "But the main thing I want to focus on right now is finding the ammunition we need to get Davey back." He laid his hands on her knees and squeezed, taking the opportunity to touch her. "You ready to get to work?"

She nodded and turned to the stack of papers. It was a woefully thin pile, considering the import of the list they were looking for.

Kyle read and reread texts. Texts about favorite foods. Texts about working out with a toddler. Texts about plans for the evening after a long day's work in the field. Nothing stood out. He tossed another sheet onto the bed in front of him, where he'd been sprawled. "I got nothing. What about you?"

She shook her head slowly then put her finger on a line. "I don't think so."

"Think? I know I haven't found anything in this section," he motioned toward his mess of papers. "If you have any doubt at all we need to look at it again."

She stood and came to the bed with a sheet in her hand. When she sat on the side, Kyle tilted toward her a little, the bed's questionable mattress giving with her insubstantial weight. She pointed to a line, "Here, Tony says something about shipments. I didn't think anything of it because it was kind of mumbo jumbo for me. It was like me discussing button versus zippers on costumes with him. I was sure he didn't care about the subject, he just let me ramble. I looked at this the same way, didn't pay much attention to it." She frowned at the readout. "I can't believe I didn't notice these before." Her expression began to lighten, "Have we found it? Have we found the list Mitchell is talking about?"

He reached for the page and read through the email then again. Tony mentioned shipments going to Afghanistan, Bahrain, and the United Arab Emirates in one email. No dates, no mention of what was on the shipment, but still. Did it breach military security?

"What was the conversation around this, Lacey?" His sheet had the tail end of the conversation.

"We were talking about how our jobs affected the world around us. I'd mentioned I worked on a lot of obscure films and didn't see a huge impact on the world. He talked about how, despite not traveling all over the world, his section was responsible for feeding and clothing soldiers all across the globe." She was silent then continued. "Now that I think about it, I remember him mentioning other countries in some posts, but would that constitute a list, in Mitchell's mind?"

He shrugged, "It may not matter, if we can convince him that's the list he's looking for. Let's give Saint and Celie a call."

When Saint answered, his tone, abrupt and cool, told Kyle more than any words could have. "What's up?"

"We have a big problem. Little Mitchell is up to a lot of shit. His daddy has been covering for him for years."

"What is it?" Lacey asked, picking up on the tension. Kyle pressed speaker, then asked Saint to repeat himself.

"What does that mean for Davey and me?" Lacey asked, her hands wrapped around her middle.

"It means DEA is going to want to control this. Celie and I are going to try to head them off so you two don't have to waste time spinning your wheels but no promises."

"Thanks. We might need them to find him, though, if we don't have any luck."

"Right. We'll see over the next twelve hours or so. You got anything?"

Lacey explained what they'd found in the emails and Celie came on, enthusiastic and willing to do some more sifting through letters. While she and Lacey discussed the list, Kyle ran through the resources he had. Saint's Brotherhood may be good at being guards and security. His organization had other skills. He glanced over at Lacey then pulled a burn phone from his backpack and turned it on. A few seconds later, his boss answered. "Yeah?"

"Hey, boss. We have a situation here. I need a backup."

Once he'd filled his employer in on the circumstances and sat through a tense question and answer session, Kyle was assured someone would be in contact with him within the hour. He disconnected only to find Lacey watching him, the now quiet cell phone in her hand. "What was that about?"

"Just calling in reinforcements," he said and tossed the phone on the bed beside him. "Let's get back to work."

Between the four of them, the team came up with a total of seven locations. Lacey listed them and then started inputting them into the computer. Kyle watched for a minute then asked, "What's up?"

She nodded toward the handwritten list. "I'm not sure. Something is there, in the back of my mind. Could you get in touch with Saint for me? I want his expertise."

When he did, Lacey asked Saint to plug in all of the countries listed and the dates around the names, which she'd jotted beside them. He disconnected and then called back within minutes. "You've hit on it, Lacey. All of these countries have bases that had deaths reported from either drug overdoses or accidental deaths. All reported within a week after supply shipments made it to the bases."

"Holy hell. This, with the photo, connects Mitchell with the drug distribution," Kyle bit out, disgust heavy in his tone.

"And according to the reports on some of the

deaths, the drugs look to have been altered in some way, making them more dangerous." Saint put in.

"If Mitchell was involved in doctoring the drugs and the bigger drug distributor gets wind of it, his ass is grass, as they say in my neck of the woods. Daddy wouldn't be able to get him out of this one." Celie added.

"So why does he need the list?" Lacey asked, "Couldn't someone with hacking skills be able to make the same connection we just did?"

"With the same information, they could. But we have the list and the dates of the shipments, which gives us a foot forward."

"Why would Tony have sent those places to Lacey?" Celie asked, her concern clear in her tone. "As far as we know he didn't have any involvement in the drug distribution or an investigation. He'd only started the questions about the shipment discrepancy right before he died."

Saint's conciliatory tone came through as he answered, "He might not have known anything more than seeing the reports in the military news, babe. You know how hard the brass is hitting, trying to address the drug issue. The lists he sent may have been unconscious, writing down those that were on the tip of his mind at the time."

Kyle nodded. "If he was involved, I think you'd have found it when you started your investigation earlier, Celie. Didn't the guy in jail spout off? He wouldn't have kept quiet if it would have saved him."

"You're probably right," Lacey could hear the doubt in Celie's voice but what could she say? She'd barely known the man.

Kyle continued, "We need to send the information to the DEA first then to Mitchell. Saint, have you heard from Patterson?"

"Yeah. We're to meet with Agent Simpson in the morning. He's the agent that was involved when we were in Kansas. He's been on the case since before we were involved but with our information, made some arrests of mid-level guys. With this information, we might be taking some steps beyond the middlemen."

"And could be stepping deeper in it," Kyle muttered.

"Yep. You need to watch your six, man."

"Ditto. You're still in it, too, man." Kyle looked to Lacey who was eying him steadily. "Keep us updated." He disconnected the call and leaned back on the bed. "You okay?"

She nodded, a flood of relief flowing through her. They'd send the information to Mitchell and finally, finally, get Davey back. "When can we send the list to Mitchell?"

"Saint will get back to me, probably within the next hour," Kyle said and stood. Lacey watched as he stretched to one side then the other, his muscles twitching and moving beneath the thin knit shirt. She didn't look away, didn't try to hide her interest. When he glanced up to find her eying him, he flushed. "Doing all that desk work can be as tiring as a workout."

"Which you're missing, right?" She could feel energy coming off him in waves.

"Yeah, it's part of my day, usually."

"Can you do some things here?" She gestured toward the questionably clean carpet.

"Not enough to count," He said and stood, then headed to his duffle, where he extracted some things then headed to the bathroom. "I'm going to take a shower. If Saint calls, let me know." He tossed her a glance over his shoulder. "I'll leave the door open a bit, just in case you need me."

She watched as he disappeared into the other room, sure he didn't have the same definition of "needing" as she did.

CHAPTER 8

THE STEAM and smell of soap wafted from the bathroom, causing a surge of awareness to run through her. She stood, stacking the papers and organizing them into some semblance of chronology. As she did, her eyes fell on the copy of the countries and dates they'd gathered together. Without Saint, Celie, and Kyle, she'd not be this close to regaining her son.

Tears gathered in her eyes and she impatiently brushed them away. She wasn't going to cry, not now, not when she was so close to victory. She pushed the papers into the folders, placed them on the desk, and turned to stare at the room.

As in all hotel rooms, the bed took precedence, its presence telling. They'd have to share that bed if they slept at all.

When the bathroom door opened and Kyle

stepped out, she turned to him. He stopped in midst of toweling his hair and stared at her. The new shirt he wore, a t-shirt this time, clung to his skin, and the jeans lovingly curled around his muscles and groin. When he didn't move, she advanced toward him and stood within inches. She could feel his heat, warming her from within.

"Thank you," She said and laid her hand on his chest.

"For what?"

"For working so hard to find the evidence we need to get Davey back. I know he's going to be with me soon." His heart beat under her hand, sure and steady, if not a little faster than when she'd first placed her palm on him.

She stepped in until her hand was the only thing separating them. "Thank you for keeping me sane, for keeping me calm. For being here."

Standing on her tiptoes, she leaned in and kissed him. His lips were firm, soft, and inviting all at the same time. As his body took her weight, Lacey knew she wanted him, wanted him to take more of her, wanted to absorb his heat. Wanted to forget the past few days and relish the time to come.

His hands went to her hips and he pulled her closer until their lower bodies connected. She shifted against his arousal, wanting to be closer.

His mouth brushed her cheek. "Lacey," he

murmured in her ear and she turned her face into his neck, breathing in his smell. The fresh soap, blended with man.

"Kyle," she responded and backed toward the bed, intent on getting prone with him on top of her. As he followed, her mind wrapped around the notion she was going to have sex for the first time since before her son was born. And it seemed very, very right.

They fell on the bed, her weight burrowing into the mattress from his body atop hers. Lacey let her legs fall apart and Kyle nestled in between them, his groin coming to rest in the V of her body. "You feel so good." He said.

"So do you," She whispered into his ear then followed it with a kiss and a small lick along the cord in his neck. His shiver told her he was as affected as she.

"Lacey." His whisper held passion, power, and something else. Regret? When his kiss didn't follow Lacey opened her eyes to see him staring at her.

He leaned over her, his arms braced on either side of her body, his face flushed and intent.

"What?"

"You don't need to do this," He said and rolled over to sit on the side of the bed.

"Do what?" Lacey tried to adjust her blouse, which had ridden up in their journey to the bed, and then sat up, her back against the headboard.

The wood, cool and impersonal against her back, served to dampen her ardor but not as much as the look Kyle sent over his shoulder.

"Show your gratitude."

"What?" Dumbfounded, she stared at him, her hands, which had been smoothing her hair back, still on her neck.

"You know. You were saying how thankful you are. How much you wanted to thank me for doing my damn job." His voice, which had started calm and flat, now rose to a near shout.

"You think because I said I was grateful you were helping me, I'd think I needed to repay you by screwing your brains out?"

"Evidence proves," he snarled.

"Evidence, hell. I wanted to say thank you because I might be seeing my son soon. I wanted to say thank you because I know you are out of your comfort zone, doing the stuff we've done over the past few days. I wanted to say thank you for being a nice guy!" She ended in her own shout then turned and pushed off the bed. "But that was my mistake. And I guess I made another mistake thinking we had a connection."

She strode into the bathroom before she started angry crying. Damn if she would let him see that, she thought as she started the water running to cover her tears.

She spent five minutes in the bathroom, taking

care of nature and washing her face. She found his comb and, with a sense of spite, ran it through her hair, leaving a couple of blonde strands in the teeth for good measure.

When she left the bathroom, Kyle was on the phone. Surprise halted her and Lacey took a breath. Maybe now, she could see Davey.

He disconnected and laid the phone on the desk. "Saint said send the photo."

Lacey found the list and clicked a picture, then sent it to Mitchell's number. Within seconds, an address and time came through and she turned to Kyle, her smile wide. "We have a time and address."

He texted Saint with the same information then they both stared at each other.

"Sorry," each said. Lacey looked down at the phone still in her hand and then at Kyle. "I didn't mean for you to misunderstand. I thought—"

"We do have a connection," he said and stepped up to her. He cupped her cheek with his hand and leaned in for a quick kiss. "When we go to bed together, I just want it to be because it's the right time for both of us."

She nodded mutely and sat at the desk, waiting for Saint's call. When he did contact them, however, it wasn't with the good news they'd hoped for.

"Damned DEA has taken over. They're doing the meet."

"Damnit!" Kyle tried to quell the sudden shard of fear thrumming through him as he thought of everything that could go wrong.

"What's happened?" Lacey asked and he relayed the change in plans.

"But isn't it okay that the DEA is involved? They're trained for this, aren't they?" She said, her face wan and pale.

"They may be trained but not to the extent I am or Saint is, for that matter. We're used to being invisible." He put the phone back to his ear. "We're going to get to be a part of it, right? Tell me they aren't that stupid."

Saint muttered a curse and confirmed Kyle's suspicions. "Agent Simpson was taken off the case. He was told he let civilians get too involved, meaning Celie and me. Now he's on the sidelines, just like we are."

"So, we go anyway," Kyle said with a touch of iron in his voice. He needed to get that boy back. If anything happened to Davey, Lacey would be destroyed.

"That's what I was thinking. Celie and I are on the way to your motel room right now. She's going to hook up with Lacey and you and I are going to let the DEA fools in on some basic truths."

Kyle discussed more plans with Saint over the phone and by the time they knocked on the motel room door, he was ready and anxious to get going.

With combined travel times of coming to the motel and making it to the meeting site, they'd be cutting it close. Too close to do real reconnaissance.

"Won't Mitchell expect me to be there?" Lacey stood at the door, blocking Kyle from exiting.

Saint stood on the other side of the entry, energy vibrating off him, just as Kyle could feel it coming from him. "They probably have a female agent who's going to act as a decoy."

"And Davey? What if he says something about the woman?" Lacey turned to look from Saint to Kyle. "I can't take the chance that he might say something, Kyle. I need to go with you."

"If she's going, I'm going," Celie said and shouldered her backpack, which she'd just slung off. She pushed a jacket into Lacey's hands and then shoved her through the door, taking Kyle with them. Shutting it, she said, "We're wasting time. Let's go."

Kyle muffled a curse as he jogged to the car. "We'll take the Charger, it has more horsepower."

Lacey and Celie clambered into the rear seats and Saint looked up directions on his phone, then passed them on. "We need to book it."

"No problem." Kyle pressed the gas pedal and kept the pressure on until he got to the interstate, where he pressed it a little more.

They were ten minutes out from the site when Kyle looked into the rearview mirror and started giving instructions. Lacey, already strung tight with anxiety, barked at him. "Don't tell me what to do, Kyle Richards. You just get to the meeting site. I'll get my son back, with your cooperation or without."

The car was silent for a second then Saint barked a laugh. "There's the wildcat mama I suspected was hiding."

Kyle didn't share in the fun. "Lacey, I'm not trying to order you around. I just want to make sure we do this as safely as possible. Let Saint and I do some scouting first, then we'll come back and give you an update."

When Celie squeezed her hand, Lacey realized she was probably being overly emotional and agreed, reluctantly. "Fine. Five minutes."

They parked the car half a mile from the site and all scrambled out. Lacey both blessed and cursed the darkness that enveloped them. The moon, shrouded by clouds, offered little light and she glanced around, looking for a building.

Saint and Kyle ushered both of the women to some shrubbery. With reassurances that Celie was well armed and Lacey well hidden, they disappeared. Try as she might, Lacey couldn't see either man after they took a step away. "How do they do that?"

"Training," Celie whispered near her ear. "They were both very good at what they were trained for."

"And that was?" Lacey asked, still searching for Kyle's big form in the gloom.

"Killing quietly." Celie's answer hung in the air.

Minutes later all hell broke loose.

Shouts followed by gunfire pulled Lacey and Celie out from their hiding spot. Her pistol at the ready, Celie led Lacey to a copse of trees, where they tucked in behind a couple of trunks. Lacey stared around the tree, taking in the madness before her. Someone was on the ground and another figure ran into a thicket, a beam of light bobbing along in front of him.

"Kyle," she whispered harshly, trying to locate him or Saint. "Davey?" Her voice became a thread of sound and she searched in vain for a tiny figure.

Saint appeared in front of them and pushed them toward the bushes. "Go! Get out of here."

"Where is Davey? Where's my son?" Lacey jerked her arm out of his grasp and wheeled to face Saint.

"He isn't here. Mitchell didn't bring him. He didn't come, either." Saint's words held a disgust she'd not heard from the gruff ex soldier. "Damn coward hired somebody to meet with you, without Davey. He was going to ambush you."

"Who was on the ground?" She asked, dreading the answer.

"The female agent." Kyle emerged from the darkness and cupped her elbow, propelling her along toward the car. She stumbled along, trying to keep up, numb.

During the walk, she registered one thing. Davey wasn't there. Was he still alive? Please God, let him be alive.

They drove back to the motel in near silence. Celie asked about the injured agent but neither Kyle nor Saint had stayed long enough to get an update. "Neither the DEA nor the hitman knew we were there and we need to keep it that way," Saint said. "We'll be more effective if we can stay invisible."

Lacey held nausea down until they made it to the motel room, then she ran to the bathroom and allowed the sickness to take over. It was better than the numbness she'd felt since she'd been told her son wasn't in the clearing.

This time, no one came to her aid, for which she was grateful. She left the bathroom to find all three of the others huddled around her phone. She held her hand out to see and Kyle handed it to her then put his arm around her.

"You bitch. Fucking DEA? Never see kid again."

CHAPTER 9

Lacey collapsed to the floor, dropping the phone. Kyle wrapped his arms around her shoulders and held on, trying to hold her together as she wept. He was vaguely aware of Saint and Celie leaving the room but cared nothing more than to hold this woman whose world was falling around her.

He picked her up and laid her on the bed, then stretched out beside her and pulled her into his arms. As he did, his brain tried to find a way to make things right. Where was the hitman? Did he have the kid? Did Mitchell? Why hadn't they tagged the last file with a cookie? How the hell were they going to find them now?

His thoughts darted around like a squirrel gathering acorns after a storm. He couldn't seem to settle on one thing to do, other than to hold Lacey.

She calmed after a few minutes, her breaths coming in sharp inhales. "I have to go," she tried to pull away but he held firm.

"You need to stay here, Lacey. We need to figure out what to do."

"I want my phone." She looked at him, her eyes stark and pain filled. "I need to text Mitchell."

He stood and found the phone on the desk and then held it out to her. What could she do wrong now? The whole affair had gone straight to hell.

He watched as she texted, "PLEASE give me my son back."

Nothing.

She repeated the plea, then folded over the phone, crying as he looked on. He raised his head when the door opened and he knew Saint and Celie could see the desolation in his expression as well. They stood at the edge of the room, as if leery of entering a sick room.

"We've called Hank," Saint said quietly. "He's talking to Agent Simpson. Maybe we'll get some answers, some direction."

Kyle nodded, "How's the agent?"

Saint knew he was referring to the female agent and shrugged. "She took a bullet to her shoulder. She'll be out of commission for a few weeks, they said. Physical therapy, recovery, so on."

Kyle stood and walked over to Saint. Celie, her face wet with tears, went and sat beside Lacey and put her arm around the other woman's shoulder. Lacey turned her head into Celie's shoulder and began to weep silently.

"We have to do something," Kyle bit out through his frustration. He was trained to take on anyone and could deal with a variety of situations. But a woman devastated and grieving a child, he couldn't take.

"What? We have no idea where Mitchell or the kid is." Saint looked almost as discouraged as Kyle felt.

"Yeah." Kyle saw the phone, now on the floor near Lacey's feet, light up. He walked over and picked it up. The readout stunned him.

"Look at this," he murmured and held the phone out to Saint. Luckily, the women were still in a clutch of grief and didn't notice them.

"Got the kid, need to exchange." Saint looked up at him. "Mitchell?" He whispered.

"Guess so, so it's probably another trick."

"One we need to confront, though." Saint looked at Lacey and then handed the phone to Kyle. "You wanta take this one?"

Kyle nodded grimly and typed. "Where?"

The address was an hour's drive and the time given allowed almost no wiggle room. "Done." He typed and put the phone in his back pocket. He glanced at Lacey, who'd raised her head to look at him.

"We got an answer." He held his hand out to her. "Let's go."

She stood and visibly pulled herself together, gathering her hair in her hands and pushing it over her shoulder then taking a deep breath. She took a step toward him and placed her hand in his. He looked down at her and said for the last time, he hoped, "We're going to get Davey back."

They drove with an eye on the clock and prayers being sent up by all silently. He pulled over a half mile from the drop off point and had Celie take over the driving. He and Saint split up and covered the ground to the meeting site in ten minutes, taking in the surrounding terrain.

Kyle pulled his gun and had it at the ready when Lacey and Celie pulled into the clearing. Low growing shrubbery didn't offer much cover, but he'd been used to less in his experience and he hunkered down, waiting. As Lacey stood, her hands wrapped around her middle, Celie paced, her eyes taking in the gloom of the early morning hours.

Fifteen minutes passed and still, Kyle hid. Saint had split up to cover the area west of the site and since then they'd texted on silent every five minutes, as agreed. Nothing had moved, other than small wildlife scurrying in the underbrush.

A car approached from the south, its lights off. Kyle inched forward, his pistol at the ready. Inside the car, a lone figure sat in the driver's seat. If it was

Mitchell, Kyle didn't know if he could restrain himself.

Lacey stood in the spotlight provided by her car's headlights. Celie had disappeared, probably covering the approaching car as well. When the car stopped several feet from Lacey, she took a step forward, only to stop at a low hiss of warning.

The driver left his car running. Unfortunate for him, as it covered any sound the men made approaching it. Saint's figure could be seen rounding the rear of the car and Kyle approached the back passenger seat and peered inside. On a blanket lay a small figure, his hands and feet bound with tape. Kyle muffled the curse he wanted to shout and found the driver, who'd opened his door.

When he started to alight from the car, Kyle stood and launched himself at the driver. He caught the guy in the back and took him down with ease, landing on his back and pinning his hands underneath him.

"Move and I'll blow your head off," he hissed in the man's ear. He glanced up at Lacey and found Celie at her side, holding her back. He said in a steady voice, "Let me get him managed and we'll go from there."

"Move off me! I ain't gonna hurt nobody." The man whined into the dirt and Kyle pulled his hands from beneath him. He realized he didn't have anything to restrain him. "Saint."

"Yeah," Saint appeared at his side, a zip tie in his hand.

"Thanks," Kyle said and quickly got the tie secured. Then he stood and opened the passenger door. Inside, still and quiet, lay a small boy.

He pulled out his pocket knife and carefully unwrapped the little legs and arms from the constraining tape. While the little guy's hands and feet felt slightly cool, Kyle couldn't see any injury. But the kid was so still.

He felt for a pulse and sent a prayer of thanks that there was one, quick and steady. When he gathered Davey into his arms and lifted him out of the car, Kyle heard Lacey's cry and her pounding feet. He took a few steps then took her weight as she crashed into him and Davey. "Let me have him," she said, her voice tight and thick.

"Let's take him over to our car. See how he is."

"Why is he asleep? Davey? Baby?"

"I didn't do anything to him. He's fine, just sleeping. Gave him a kid's sleeping pill." The driver, now standing, not Mitchell, was all about giving information. As Saint and Celie stood on either side of him, he rushed to fill them in.

Kyle's attention was split between Davey and Lacey and the story the driver, who'd refused to give his name, was providing. "Creep wanted me to do the kid. I don't kill kids. I ain't going to do no kid. No way."

"How'd you get the phone number to text us?" Celie said, her face set and ruthless in the shadow the car's headlights made. Saint was texting someone on his phone, Kyle noted. The police? Hank?

"Got it from Mitchell's phone. Fool doesn't watch as close as he should. Left the cell laying on the table."

"And what about the earlier drop point? You the guy he sent before?"

All of a sudden, the cooperative man of earlier was gone and he'd been replaced with a mute. Celie and Saint's attempts at questioning him further ended in nothing more than glares and wriggling at the restraints. He even tried running when another black SUV pulled up to the clearing. Boomer Rayne got out and sauntered up to the group. "Busy night, Saint?"

"Not so much. Kyle and I have a present for the cops. You might let them know to check out the car for some weapons. And the DEA agent who was shot? Might be a connection with this guy."

"Who is he?" Boomer asked, his expression curious.

"No name but he's an associate of Grayson Mitchell, Jr.," Celie said. "And do us a favor before you connect with the cops, will you? Check and see if there's any evidence of a child in the car. We don't want to share that information yet."

Boomer gave all of them a long look, especially Kyle and Lacey, who cradled her son to her. After a long moment, he nodded and took over. Another man who'd been in the car came and started policing the area, removing footprints, evidence of surveillance, and anything that might pull in Kyle and his crew's presence.

On the way back to the motel, Lacey said, her voice quiet and reverent as she stared at her son. "Why'd you want them to hide us being there, getting Davey back?" she whispered.

He wasn't sure why he'd wanted the team kept shadowed, other than to provide an element of surprise if they needed it. Plus, the lack of publicity couldn't hurt. When he explained the reasons to her, Lacey didn't argue or prevaricate. Instead, she cuddled her son closer and leaned into Kyle's side, almost unconsciously, he thought.

A buzz on Saint's phone alerted them as they pulled into the motel. He waited until he'd parked and then hustled everyone into the room. "We may still have a problem."

Kyle watched as Celie and Lacey hovered around Davey, looking him over for any signs of abuse or harm. When he turned to Saint, he caught the man looking on at the women as well, an expression of adoration in his eyes. Kyle wondered, was he guilty of the same?

"What's up?" he came to stand beside the other man and looked at the text.

"Boomer is one of the Brotherhood's best. I had him drive over here in case we needed him. He's questioned our guy. Driver is Jerry Bernard. Low life criminal for hire, does whatever gets him money. He says Mitchell has a boner for getting rid of all of you, especially Lacey. Has put out feelers to have her killed. Watch your six." Saint looked up from the text with a worried expression.

"Damnit!" Kyle hissed. "Is this guy stupid as well as careless?"

"We've all but eliminated the charges of kidnapping by not reporting it after the initial event, Kyle. And with us staying under the radar, he doesn't have anything to answer to, other than the possible drug charges. And Daddy might be able to get him out of it, again."

Kyle cursed. Senator Mitchell had been instrumental in getting his son out of one after the other situations, including drunk driving, drug use charges, and other distasteful events in the man's life. Now, though, with the DEA involved, maybe they could get him charged and tried. "Is Agent Simpson to be trusted?"

"I think so, he seemed okay when Celie and I had business with him. But someone tipped off Mitchell about the DEA bust and no one else knew about it, other than the Brotherhood. Simpson thinks there may be a mole in the agency."

Kyle glanced back at Lacey, who'd picked up her now drowsy son and was heading toward the bathroom. "We need to find a way to end this, Saint. She can't take much more and Davey may not survive the next attempt."

"I agree," Saint said, his voice taut. "We need some help, though."

Kyle smiled grimly. "I know just the guy."

CHAPTER 10

LACEY DRESSED Davey in the set of clothes Celie had procured for him, a tiny shirt with a car on it and jeans. His eyes, still at half-mast, turned blearily on her. "Mommy?"

"It's me, baby. You okay?"

"Bad man, Mommy. No more bad man." Davey's head lolled to the side and she wondered if she should take him to the doctor. He'd slept through the hour's drive to the motel and mostly through the bath. Now, he tried to talk and look around, but his eyes kept sliding shut.

She turned to see Kyle in the doorway. "How is he?"

She stood from where she'd been seated on the closed toilet and held Davey, his head on her shoulder. "He's still really groggy. I'm wondering if I should take him to the ER."

Kyle stood to the side and then followed her into the room. She sat on the bed and put her son down beside her, his small frame tucked into her side.

"Who's he?"

Lacey glanced down to see Davey's brown gaze fixed on Kyle. Kyle in turn was watching Davey as if he'd never seen a toddler before. Maybe he hadn't, at least in his adulthood. "That's our friend, Kyle. He helped me find you."

"Good man?" Davey leaned away from her slightly, examining the tall man standing at the edge of the bed.

"Yes."

"Play cars?" Davey asked, offering the best form of friendship he could think of.

"I like to play with them. But my cars are bigger, I think, than yours." Kyle appeared to give serious thought to the topic.

"Cars in pocket." Davey scrambled clumsily to his feet and Lacey held onto his back to help him. He put his hands in his pockets then frowned, "Mommy, cars."

"Your cars are at home, honey. We'll buy you some to play with here, okay?" Lacey would have bought her son a Ferrari right now if he wanted it. Instead, he smiled and nodded, then started playing with the television remote. She quickly took the device from him, fearful of what the small motel offered in the way of entertainment, and found a kid's channel. Soon, Davey was seated in the middle of the bed, his thumb in his mouth and his gaze fixed on the shark cartoon.

She watched him for a minute, sad to see the thumb sucking. He'd outgrown the habit a few months ago, but now it had returned. Hopefully, that would be the only holdover from this experience.

"He okay?" Kyle asked quietly, his eyes on her son.

"I think so. He's awake now, at least." She looked at the crack in the curtains at the milky dawn breaking. "And I'm exhausted," she breathed, holding back a yawn.

"Take a nap. I'll run out and pick up some food in a couple of hours. He's bound to be hungry by then."

She nodded and laid back, pulling the sheet over her. Her last sight was of her son bobbing to the cartoon soundtrack.

An hour later, she woke to his laughter. Celie, seated at the desk, had Davey on her lap and was bouncing him up and down, singing a song in Spanish. Davey, his face alight with joy, watched her and moved his mouth in time with hers. When Lacey sat up, her hair in her eyes and her blouse twisted around her torso, Celie halted in her song and sent her a wry smile. "Sorry. I guess I got carried away."

"That's okay. He seems to like it. What is it?"

"Just a song about elephants on a spider web. My mother used to sing it to my brother and me when we were young." Celie looked at Lacey. "Davey doesn't speak Spanish, does he?"

Lacey swallowed a spurt of guilt at the question and shook her head. "I hadn't really thought about it, Celie. I should have, I know."

"It's not too late. He's still young enough to pick it up fast. Aren't you, Davey?" She waggled him from side to side, eliciting another chuckle.

Lacey got out of the bed and glanced around the room. "Where's Kyle?"

"He and Luc went to pick up some food. I also asked them to get some essentials for Davey. Underpants, pullups, a couple of T-O-Ys as well." She shrugged, "I didn't want to wake you to ask what he was wearing so they're covering all the bases."

"He was in underpants, but with everything that's been going on, he might regress a little. He was sucking his thumb when I laid down and he hasn't done that in months."

"He's a resilient little thing, you know? He took right to me and hasn't blinked an eye with Luc's arm." Celie hummed the song and Davey bounced along, his eyes on his mother.

"Sing, Mama." He commanded with a smile.

"Oh, no, baby. You don't want me to sing right now. Mama's going to go take a shower if Aunt Celie will watch you for a few minutes." At Celie's nod, Lacey retrieved her clothes and retreated to the shower. She surprised herself with a cry during the few minutes she allowed herself away from her son. From relief? It had to be. She had Kyle, Saint, and Celie to thank for Davey's safe return. Now she had to find a way to keep him safe. No more chances. No more adventures.

No more Kyle.

She paused in the act of rinsing her hair and thought about that. No more Kyle? He was the kind of man who thrived on action and thrills. Wasn't that what he did for a living, taking chances? No, no matter how he made her feel, the surge of awareness that charged through her at his touch, she couldn't afford to take any more chances with Kyle Richards.

She finished her shower and quickly dried off then dressed. When she stepped out of the bathroom, her hair wrapped in a towel, Lacey found the others grouped around the small table with fast food breakfast platters spread around. Davey, still seated on Celie's lap, was eating a chunk of pancake with his hands. Lacey arched an eyebrow at his aunt who shrugged. "I'm not Mama. I can let him get away with this."

Davey waved the pancake at Lacey. "Bite, Mama?"

She smiled and shook her head ruefully. "No thanks, honey. Your Aunt Celie is going to let you eat all that syrupy goodness. And after that, she can help out with your bath."

Saint snorted a laugh at Celie's expression. "You asked for that, babe."

She tossed a tater tot at him, eliciting a giggle from Davey. Kyle, sitting slightly apart from the group, looked mystified at the casualness and apparent joy. "Do all aunts act like you?"

"Don't know," Celie said and deftly plopped a tater tot in her mouth. "Never met any other aunts."

"Some do, some don't," Lacey said, opening another platter to find eggs, bacon, and toast in hers. As she found a packet of salt and started seasoning her food, she added. "I had a great aunt who was so much fun, but we got into a lot of trouble when she visited too."

"Like what?" He asked, taking a sip of black coffee, a breakfast sandwich on a napkin in front of him.

"Oh, things like getting hot pink nail polish on my bedspread, eating ice cream for breakfast, things like that. She also told me about sex when I was thirteen, which made my mom furious." Lacey grinned. "Although when I asked Mom what she was so upset about, Aunt Shea said she'd told her about sex too."

"Sounds like you had a pretty cool aunt," Celie said, and when Davey lunged for his mother, released him. Lacey took her slightly sticky son and turned him so he could start eating from her tray. He poked at the eggs with the end of the plastic fork then started to grab a handful. She intervened, blocking his hand and took the fork then helped him shovel some in his mouth. When he reached for a slice of toast, she gave him a small piece and let him chew on it.

Kyle watched as she deftly but gently led her son through the process of feeding himself. When did kids start learning that? And didn't they just pick it up? Kyle wondered at the things parents had to do to teach kids.

He ate the rest of his sandwich and downed his coffee before opening another one.

"Bite?" He lifted his head to find a small hand holding a piece of minced potato out to him. Kyle started to automatically reject the food. It was being held by a hand that had gone through at least three other foods and probably been in the kid's mouth as well. But when he looked into those brown eyes, then his mother's blue ones, Kyle found himself leaning forward and slowly closing his mouth over the morsel. Lacey's smile, radiant and a little misty, made the slightly moist bite worth it all.

"Thanks, bud." He smiled and held out a small bite of his sausage and cheese wrap. "You want a bite?"

Davey's bird mouth, open wide, charmed him and he fed him several bites. When Davey pointed to Kyle's second cup of coffee and said "Drink?", however, Lacey called an end to his communal meal.

"No need for more energy, honey. Let's get you cleaned up." When Celie offered to assist, Lacey shook her head. "I want to do this on my own for now. But next time you let him eat syrup with his hands, you definitely get bath duty."

"Deal," Celie replied.

After Lacey disappeared into the bathroom with Davey and the myriad of new supplies they'd purchased, Kyle turned to Saint. "I called a buddy of mine. He's on his way."

"How long before he gets here?" Saint started bagging the meals and Celie stood then retrieved a couple of backpacks. From one she retrieved Saint's laptop and from the other, her spiral notebook and pen. By the time she'd done this, the table was cleared and Davey was in the middle of the bed, making sputtering noises with little cars. Lacey looked around at the other adults. "What's going on?"

Kyle leaned back in his chair. "Mitchell has contacted people. He wants us all eliminated, but you especially."

She whirled and looked at her son, who, thankfully was entertained by the cartoons on the television and his toys. When she turned back around, her expression was fierce. "No. Not again. I won't let him hurt my son, ever."

Kyle didn't correct her assumption it was Davey Mitchell was aiming for. If she thought that, then she'd be more likely to agree to his plan. Risky, hell yeah. But necessary, if she was ever to find peace.

"We're not going to let that happen. I have a buddy coming down. Boomer, from the Brotherhood, is staying close by too. We'll have a plan within the hour." He turned to glance at Saint and Celie, who were hunched over the laptop. "We'll take care of you and Davey, I promise."

CHAPTER 11

SETH ISSACS WAS A BIG GUY, with blond hair and a faint stubble. His expression, though, was one that Lacey would never want to see in a man she just met. He looked like he could eat shards of glass and enjoy it, if need be.

"We're set." He said, his tone flat and even. He'd not responded in either a friendly or adversarial fashion when he met Lacey and Davey. In fact, she wondered if he even registered their existence, other than as elements of the mission. This man made Kyle look like a warm teddy bear.

Davey sat on her lap, his thumb in his mouth and his eyes huge. While Celie and Saint chatted with Boomer, a handsome dark-haired man, over in the corner, Issacs and Kyle went over a bag of what they called essentials. It looked like the entire inventory of a gun store, with some knives and rope thrown in for good measure. Lacey turned away, suddenly cold.

Kyle was doing this for her. Taking yet another chance in protecting her. She'd put so many people at risk and cost an agent an injury in the course of searching for her son. While she'd do it over again, she regretted putting anyone else in harm's way.

"Are you okay?" Celie asked as she sat next to Lacey and handed Davey a truck. He took the toy but didn't attempt to play with it. His eyes remained on the two men busy with their grown-up toys.

"I'm tired of this, Celie. Tired of being scared, tired of putting people at risk." She sighed. "I just want to go home and be my old boring self."

Celie's smile held a touch of sadness. "You'll never be the same, you know. Even if you go back to Seattle, work in the theater, and raise Davey without another emergency or problem cropping up. This," she waved her hand around the room, taking in all of the action. "All of this will change you, just like being in the military changed all of us."

Lacey sighed. She knew it would change her, had already done so. And her son? Would it make him more fearful of people, of doing things? Only time and her attention to his life would tell.

Saint held his hand up and motioned the group

to him. Lacey, still holding Davey, joined them at the outer edge of the crowd around the computer.

"I just got a message from Hank. There does seem to be someone leaking information to Mitchell. Since we know you hadn't had any communication with the other Shadow Ops people before you contacted Seth, it's not your organization, Kyle. That leaves the Brotherhood and the DEA." Saint frowned and sent them all a disgusted look. "Hank's on a tear about the possibility someone in the Brotherhood could be at fault. And Agent Simpson is up in arms, too."

"So, the upshot is we have to do this thing on our own," Seth said, nodding his head. "No problem."

"But it also means we'll be on our own with the locals," Boomer said, his expression dark.

"Yep. We go in dark, stay dark and then hand over the contract man to who? Do we just tie him up and leave him sitting?" Celie's voice held the same frustration all of them were feeling.

Lacey turned away from them and walked to the bed where she found a kid's show on the television. She put Davey on the bed, promising herself when they got home the television would be off limits for both of them for a month. After she was convinced her son was absorbed enough to turn her attention elsewhere, she addressed the group.

"We need to stop this." When they all started talking, she held her hand up.

"Look. It's obvious Mitchell is being protected by someone, his father, an organization, his wealth. Whatever. I'm convinced that, no matter what we do, we'll not be able to catch him."

She started pacing the room, her thoughts coalescing into something she hadn't had in months. Controlled thought. "I want to talk to Mitchell myself. No intermediaries, no body-guards. No one but us." She turned to Celie, her voice firm and steady. "I want you and Saint to take Davey home with you."

"What? What are you talking about?" Celie said, her voice rising to a pitch Lacey had never heard before.

"She's giving up," Kyle said, his tone flat.

She turned on him, her face feeling hot. "I'm not giving up. I'm facing facts. We have what, six people, against a person who has bought off an organization? A man who has connections we don't even know about? I don't want anyone else hurt because of me, I can't have it." She finished with a near shout.

Kyle advanced on her, his face a bit flushed too. "And when he comes after you? Sends his henchman to kill you? What then? Are you going to let Celie and Saint raise your son? Or are you going to spend the rest of your life running?" He put his hands on her shoulders and stared at her intently. "I promised you I'd take care of you. Don't you believe me?"

She leaned into his touch, her defenses crumbling at the look in his eyes. "I know you'll try. Even to the point that you die for me. But I can't deal with that. And after you're gone, or after the first man is eliminated or arrested, what then? Mitchell will just hire someone else."

"She has a point." Boomer quietly asserted.

Kyle released her shoulders but when she started to step away from him, Lacey found her hand enfolded in his. Boomer, his huge frame squeezed into one of the desk chairs and his arms folded over his chest. "She's right. There's always someone ready to do something for money. If Mitchell is willing to pay, he can find someone to take her out."

"So, we don't go for the henchmen. We go for Mitchell." Kyle said.

"And what then?" Lacey said, tired of arguing with them all. "He's got one of the most powerful men in Washington as a father and obviously has deep pockets."

They all stood, staring at her for a minute, then Boomer said quietly, "We call in Agent Simpson. He's law enforcement and he's not the mole. He can make the arrests."

"And we accept Lacey's offer," Seth quietly

stated, causing them all to turn to look at him. He sat on the edge of the bed, turning one of Davey's trucks in his hand, staring at it. When he looked up, he smiled at her, his face turning from the stone-cold killer she suspected he was to that of an extremely attractive man, someone who could charm and beguile. "We use her as bait and get Mitchell where he's most vulnerable. His ego."

KYLE PULLED his pistol from his holster and fired off four rounds. He'd cussed, fussed, and generally made an ass of himself during the past day. No one, other than Boomer, who'd laughed at him, had responded. Lacey, who was spending her time with her son exclusively, had not even made eye contact with him over supper the night before. When Celie had suggested getting steak dinners for everyone, an air of celebration had taken over the group, just like it had been pre-mission in the old days.

Except Lacey had viewed the meal as her last supper, he mused. She'd given Davey her fries, letting him eat them almost to the exclusion of any green vegetables. She'd picked at the other food on her plate and had even rejected the glass of wine Celie had poured her. Now, with her at the motel with Davey, Kyle had to face the fact that she was divorcing herself from them all.

"I found a handwritten will," Saint muttered as he stepped up to Kyle's side.

"Lacey?"

Saint nodded grimly. "She's convinced it's going to end badly."

"We have to prove otherwise," Kyle said and checked his gun again before aiming at the target tacked to the tree trunk one hundred yards away. The earlier ones, closer in, had been decimated by the two men.

"And if we don't?"

"She's gone," Kyle said, his stomach churning.

Saint sent off several rounds, cursed, repeated the action, and nodded grimly before turning to Kyle. "You need to fix that, you know."

"What?" Kyle said, intent on cleaning his pistol.

"Her leaving."

"If it's her decision, I need to respect that."

"Even if it's not what either of you want?"

Kyle huffed a breath and turned away, holstering his gun and walking to the bench where his jacket lay. By the time he'd put it on Saint was by his side, his own weapon open and gleaming in the sun. Saint dropped onto the bench and took up the oiled rag Kyle had tossed to the bench and started rubbing his pistol. His attention on the gun, he continued. "She's trying to be noble and brave when she's scared shitless, you know."

"But she's also a woman who's thinking of her

son," Kyle said, slouching on the bench, welcoming the bite of the rough wood on his shoulders.

"She's willing to give up a lot for the ones she loves, yes. And that includes you, you know." When Kyle turned to stare at Saint in surprise, the other man grinned. "She didn't say anything about me or Boomer getting killed, did she? Or that Celie or Seth was at risk? Nope. Just you and Davey." Saint stood and shoved his gun into his back holster then tossed the rag into his duffel, which he shouldered. As he started walking away, he threw over his shoulder. "I'd not let Celie go if she talked about me dying."

Kyle shook his head at the man's logic and followed him to the car. Was he right, though? Was the reason Lacey was so intent on going through with this insane plan of Seth's that she cared for him, beyond that of a civilized person?

Agent Simpson arrived at the motel the next day. His arrival made the small room officially too crowded and Lacey retreated to the room Celie and Saint had taken next door. As she closed the door behind her, she thought of the crowd of SUVs and their lone muscle car in the parking lot. It was probably the most traffic this small motel had seen in a while.

Davey, finally calm and content to play with the ever-expanding car and truck collection he'd been gifted with, sat on the bed, pillows forming his hills and race tracks. She sat at the desk area, her laptop open in front of her, typing instructions and a journal for her son. When the task became too morbid, even for her state of mind, she closed the laptop and took up one of Celie's ever present notebooks. Finding a pen, Lacey started scribbling and drawing. Within minutes, she had a fair rendering of Kyle and Davey. Last night, when she'd come from the shower, he'd been on the bed, sprawled on his side and chugging away with a tiny dump truck in his hand. Davey, equally sputtering with his tongue protruding from his lips, was following along with a fire truck. When Kyle found her watching, he'd grinned. "I forgot how much fun this was."

If she'd not realized it before, she knew then her heart was his. But he'd never find that out, she promised herself. He couldn't know how she felt about him. Not with the plan she had in place. They'd slept in the bed with Davey between them, not touching but for her, his presence had made for a night of cat naps and longing for what couldn't be.

A knock on the door brought her around and she tossed the notebook down before checking the peephole. Celie stood on the other side of the door, fairly dancing in step. When Lacey opened the door, the other woman came inside with a bag from a local chain store. "I found a little racetrack," she crowed and held up the bag.

"He's too small." Lacey laughed helplessly. Whenever anyone went for supplies, another truck or car ended up in Davey's little hands. He'd come to expect to be able to rifle through a bag when someone brought one in and this time was no exception. In an instant, he'd scrambled down from the bed and ran to Celie. "Truck?"

"Nope. Cars. And a road." Celie reached into the bag and removed a cardboard box that held larger, toddler-sized cars and a connecting raceway. As she advanced into the room, she said over her shoulder, "Kyle wants to talk to you in the other room. I'll watch Davey."

"Okay," Lacey smoothed her hair down and stepped next door.

CHAPTER 12

THE ROOM she'd shared with Kyle was oddly quiet. Lacey glanced around only to find a stack of notebooks and papers, thanks to Celie, resting beside a closed laptop. The only other evidence of visitors was a full garbage can, topped off with Styrofoam coffee cups. She stepped inside and closed the door behind her. "Kyle?"

He came out of the bathroom, a towel around his shoulders and his chest bare. A sprinkling of light brown hair dusted his pecs. Lacey's eyes trailed down his chest to his stomach, then the lean double lines of muscle that framed his lower abdomen. His jeans braced his lean hips and she swallowed at the surge of longing the whole picture of him presented.

"You okay?" His voice, normally even and of a smooth timbre, sounded rough and low.

Lacey nodded then stepped a few feet into the room. "Celie said you wanted to see me. Where are the others?"

He tossed the towel in the general direction of the bathroom and started forward, coming in on her. Lacey'd never felt endangered or uncomfortable with Kyle and didn't now. But she definitely felt a little crowded when he stopped mere inches away from her.

"They've gone out scouting."

"All of them?" She squeaked as he reached up and brushed a lock of her hair over her shoulder.

"Uh huh. Felt like we might need some time to talk." He reached down and took her hand then towed her farther into the room. Lacey moved with him, aware he was planning more than a conversation.

"Talk? What is there to talk about?"

He sat on the edge of the bed and pulled her down to join him. When she perched on the very edge, he leaned back on both elbows, displaying his lean body to the best advantage. Had he planned that? She wondered as she swallowed the sudden longing to taste that narrow line of hair that went from his navel down into the jeans.

"We need to clear the air between us."

"About?"

"Feelings," he shifted his weight and brought his hand to hers, pulling her down onto her side.

She rolled to her back, her head turned toward him.

"Feelings."

"And the future," he added, turning onto his side to face her. His hand went into the gap between her shirt and pants and he smoothed it along her stomach. She shivered at the slight roughness in his fingers. Fingers that were experienced in secrecy.

"We've talked about the future, Kyle. A lot."

"No, you've talked about it. You haven't heard my version of the future. A life with you, me, and Davey in it." His hand smoothed across her skin again, this time with a small finger dipping past her waistband. Another shudder ran through her, a heated quiver that started in her chest and radiated through her core.

"We don't know each other well enough to have a future together, Kyle. And you want something I don't." She tried to shift away from him, or at least she thought about it. Her body, however, wouldn't follow the edicts her mind sent.

"We've gotten to know the essentials about each other these past few days," he said and inched closer, his body now touching her side from shoulder to hip. He leaned in and started to nibble her ear. "I know you would move heaven and earth for the people you love. You're brave and strong but aren't afraid of showing your emotions. You don't trust easily but when you do, you give all your faith wholeheartedly. And you love, you love with your whole being."

His kiss, soft and warm, brought her heart to a standstill and Lacey turned into him, giving him what he asked for. She opened her mouth to his exploration and then gave in to the urge to explore a little on her own. Her hands, which had been at her side, found their way around his waist, then his back. The bisecting line down the center seemed to call her to explore and when she found a ticklish spot on his shoulder blade, she made him lay on his stomach so she could delve into the study of laughter and licking.

Kyle gave her exquisite pleasure, taking time to explore, touch, and taste. His hands and mouth became one source of pleasure and by the time he ranged his large body over hers and entered her, Lacey was immersed in a world of sensation.

Later, as they lay on the bed, facing each other she smiled and said, "You're quite the Romeo, you know."

He laughed and then rolled to his stomach, his arm over her belly. "I've been accused of it a time or two." He turned serious then, "But this time, I mean it, Lace. I want us to be together."

She sighed and stared at a slightly darkened spot on the ceiling near the light fixture. "And what you do for a living? Would you be willing to give that up?"

He stilled. Where she felt constant movement, energy, she now sensed blankness, as if a part of his consciousness separated them at her words.

She turned to look at him. "The last few months have been hell for me, Kyle. I don't like taking chances, not with my life or Davey's. I don't like worrying about danger, about someone being out there hating me and wanting to hurt me or my son."

"And you think my job would increase those odds?" He didn't pull away from her but she suddenly felt cold. His arm, earlier a source of pleasure and stability, now felt like dead weight across her stomach.

"No, but I'd be worried all the time about you. About the situations you were in." She felt a tear roll down her cheek as she stared at him, his handsome face. She brought her hand up to caress his bearded chin. "I don't know how we could make it work."

When he rolled away from her, she stifled the urge to pull him back into her embrace. To beg him not to go, not to abandon her. But she'd asked him to, hadn't she? She'd ended the love affair of a lifetime before it could even begin.

KYLE STOOD at the bedside and pulled on his pants, his back to Lacey. She scrambled from the bed and retrieved her clothes then disappeared into the bathroom. Well, that had gone to hell, he thought as he tucked his shirt into his jeans and zipped them up. All of his grand plans of romancing her and convincing her life with him was worth taking a chance on. Now, she'd decided never to take another chance in life at all.

He ignored the rumpled bed as he went to the table and retrieved his phone. A few taps and he'd sent a text to Saint, letting him know it was all clear. The whole scene had been Saint's idea. "Show her how you feel about her. Let her in, Kyle. She might surprise you."

And she had, indeed, shocked him. He'd thought of possibilities like she'd reject his affection, not be as attracted to him as he was to her. She'd tell him she didn't want a relationship because she wasn't sure how he'd be with her son. She'd not want a long-distance relationship. He'd been prepared for all of those possibilities. But to say she didn't want to take a chance on him and his lifestyle? That hadn't been on his radar.

When she exited the bathroom, she looked as if she'd been crying but he doubted he'd affected her as much as that. He wondered at his mood; it was as if he were a kid that had been told he couldn't play shortstop during the game. He was hurt!

He turned away from her, stunned at the intensity of the rejection. All he wanted to do right now was to leave, get away from her. Do something other than stay in this damned motel room with her.

Celie knocked on the door and when he opened it, sent him a sheepish smile. "Davey wanted his mom. I think he's ready for a nap." She had the little boy in her arms, his head bobbing on his shoulders.

"Tired, little guy?" Kyle automatically reached out for him and to his surprise, Davey leaned away from Celie and wrapped his arms around Kyle's neck. When he tucked his head into the curve of Kyle's shoulder, the pain of Lacey's rejection both eased and intensified. Her refusal to accept his love also meant he'd lose Davey.

Lacey stood, her hands at her side, her expression stark and pain filled. He held her son, feeling the warm soft puffs of breath moisten his neck.

"He's asleep," Celie whispered and then leaned in and closed the door behind her, leaving the three of them alone.

Kyle advanced and nodded toward the bed. When Lacey didn't move, he murmured, "Turn down the covers, will you?" She did and he lowered Davey to the bed, then removed the tiny sneakers and socks, finally covering him with the sheet. When he straightened, Lacey's eyes were filled with tears. She turned away from him and started straightening stuff in the room.

"I need to go over some notes," he said, making

an excuse to get as far away as he could while he was still in the same room. She nodded, her back to him, and sat at the desk, a notebook in front of her, a pen in her hands.

The next fifteen minutes were silent, the sounds of turning pages, a scritch of a pen on paper, and the sound of her son's breathing filling the void.

SHE SENT the message that evening. Expecting a response within the hour, Lacey spent her time with Davey, playing with him, singing songs with him, and learning some snippets of Spanish with him, alongside Celie. She tried not to think beyond the moment, the time she had with her son. And Kyle? He spent his time with the other men, planning, going over their notes and surveillance information.

"It didn't go so well with Kyle, did it?" Celie's quiet comment forced Lacey's attention away from the dark thoughts in her head.

"You might say that."

"He doesn't want a kid around?"

Lacey looked up, surprised at the question. "No, he didn't mention Davey at all. I don't think he even thought about it."

"So, what was his problem?" Celie's tone implied it was all about Kyle, not Lacey's decisions.

"It wasn't Kyle." Lacey returned.

"But you—" Lacey's shook her head, letting Celie know it wasn't something she wanted to pursue. They played along with Davey for a few minutes more before her phone pinged, indicating a message coming through.

Agent Simpson, who'd been coordinating the strike, came to stand beside her and read over her shoulder. "You come alone. No one else." An address followed.

"Damnit, he's changed locations," Simpson grated out and Lacey looked up at him in surprise.

"Did you think he'd use the same place as before? He may be a lousy human being, Agent, but he's clearly not stupid."

Several stifled coughs and snickers met her comment and she turned to take in the men before her. "I'm sure all of you are confident in your skills, and I'm equally so. But here's the thing. Mitchell isn't going to take anything for granted, other than the fact that he's going to win. It's up to all of us to make sure that doesn't happen."

When all the men looked at her in surprise, save Simpson, who hadn't been privy to her pity party earlier, she continued. "I know I've been less than courageous lately and I'd decided I was going to have to sacrifice myself. I've changed my mind." She smiled at Celie who was holding Davey. "I want to see my son's children and even his grandchildren.

And I'm not going to go into this quietly like a lamb." She took in all of them.

"We have six hours to find out everything there is to learn about this new location. And to get me ready to meet Mitchell." She focused on Kyle for the first time since they'd argued. Since they'd made love. "And I want to come out of this alive."

Celie and Saint got to work, contacting Hank and then one of the other Brotherhood computer gurus to help with research into Mitchell, his cronies, and his recent activity. Simpson spent his time going over his case, rehashing bits and pieces of the drug distribution lists. He'd tied several of the locations and times to dates Mitchell had been in transit with his father. The question, he said with his teeth clenched, was whether the senior Mitchell as in it up to his neck as well.

When Simpson mentioned the injured agent, Lacey asked how she was doing. Simpson shook his head, "Not good. She got some kind of infection after she was released. I haven't heard anything more, since I've been limiting my communications with the agency."

Lacey silently cursed Mitchell. If this agent died, there would be yet another life he'd destroyed in addition to the countless men and women who'd fallen prey to drugs.

Kyle divided his time between counseling her on evasive maneuvers and preparing a strike force with Seth and Saint. Boomer also helped with the training. When Lacey asked about defensive measures, both men shook their heads. "You've been injured and aren't working at full strength. Besides, it takes years to train to be an effective fighter."

She scoffed. "I don't want to fight. I just want to be able to get out of a clinch or to give him a taste of his own. Surely there's something you can teach me."

Kyle sighed and glanced over to Celie, who'd taken a break and had Davey by the hand, heading for the bathroom. "Celie, you got a few minutes to go over some basic defensive measures with Lacey?"

"Maybe later," she said airily. "I've got to take Davey to the bathroom."

When Lacey apologized for not noticing her son's needs, Celie waved her hand. "It's fine. We're his village."

Kyle turned back to her, his green eyes quiet and searching. "We'll go next door, get some basics down. Maybe you can practice with her later, feel more comfortable with her."

She nodded, her heart suddenly beating faster. She definitely wasn't feeling comfortable with him right now. Wanting to jump his bones despite knowing she couldn't have a future with him wasn't comfortable. Knowing she'd have to touch him and he would do likewise, wasn't comfortable. But she needed him, wanted him to train her. "I trust you," She said quietly and he nodded then led her to the other room.

Thirty painful minutes later, she had a couple of basic moves to get out of a hold, assuming she could keep her head. She took a breath and rubbed her still sore side.

"Did I hurt the stitches?" Kyle asked, his breath irritatingly steady.

"No, it just stings some." She removed her hand and lifted her chin. "Let's continue."

CHAPTER 13

THE AREA MITCHELL had chosen was a parking lot, open and without any areas to use as cover. Kyle cursed as he looked at the image on the computer. "We'll have to use scopes."

He hadn't used a scoped rifle in a mission in a couple of years. Sure, he practiced regularly, but he hadn't had to depend on his skills lately. Now, everything rode on his abilities to hit a small, probably moving target.

Saint nodded and pulled a case from the SUV's cargo area. They were parked five miles away from the meeting site and had been in place for fifteen minutes, trying to review the plans. What had been a crowded business district was now deserted lots with very little security. Swede, one of Hank Patterson's most trusted men, had found a way to hack into outside security cameras in the designated lot and was monitoring activity, as well as recording it for future use.

"We have movement," Celie said quietly, her post in the SUV's rear seat covered with computer equipment. Saint and Kyle, as well as Boomer stepped forward to peer at the screen. Two vehicles, one a black luxury sedan and the other an older pickup truck, pulled into the lot. As all of them looked on the cars pulled up next to each other, the driver's sides facing.

"What are they doing?" Kyle asked.

"Probably talking," Boomer said, his voice low as if someone might be listening. All of them were dressed in black tactical gear and armed to the teeth.

Kyle glanced over at the other car. Davey, asleep in the rear seat, hopefully would remain unaware of his mother's movements this night. Kyle sent up a rare prayer that the kid would have a whole parent at the end of all this and the nightmare he'd had to live through would be over.

"We need to head out," he said, his voice tight with tension. Seth stepped up beside him and, with a single nod, then stepped away and headed to another SUV. Kyle joined him and Boomer filled the back seat. Saint and Celie had reluctantly agreed to stay behind with Davey, though Kyle noted Celie embracing Lacey and giving her an intense look at the decision.

They drove within a mile of the meeting site and started dispersing. As he took up a slow jog, Kyle glanced at his watch. Five minutes from now, Lacey would get in another vehicle and drive to the parking lot, alone. He hoped like hell that Mitchell wasn't smart enough to have an ambush set up between them and the meeting point. If so, Lacey wouldn't stand a chance.

He took his position at the edge of the lot, behind a dumpster, and silently fell into old habits. He ignored the pebbles he lay on, the odd twinge in his spine from bending his back to gaze around the large boxy structure. As he stared through the viewfinder in his scope, he located the pickup truck, parked behind a clump of bushes on the west end of the lot. He then found the driver, crouch walking to another scrawny bush. The guy looked to be about fifty, out of shape, and with a basic hunting rifle in his hands. While Kyle would never underestimate a skilled amateur, neither was he in any doubt he could and would take the man out if Lacey was in imminent danger.

Simpson, on the other end of the parking lot, had given instructions not to kill. If necessary, injury would be acceptable, but with the need to stay covert, as well as the fact that all of them, save Simpson, were civilians, no one would escape investigations in this scenario. Hell with that, Kyle thought as he watched Lacey drive into the parking lot.

She pulled to a spot under a weak security light, its artificial yellow gleam tinting the whole vehicle. From Kyle's perspective, he could see her head and shoulders, but nothing else.

She'd agreed not to get out of the car, but to wait for Mitchell so when her door opened five minutes later, he cursed and started moving toward her. The sound of clicks in his earpiece told him someone, probably Simpson, was pissed at his movements but he couldn't let her meet Mitchell alone.

Mitchell stepped from a darkened area on the south end, opposite Kyle's position. His awkward hold on the pistol demonstrated his lack of experience. That could be dangerous if he got close enough to do some damage.

"Keep down, damnit. If he sees you, he'll run." Simpson hissed into his earpiece. Kyle didn't bother to reply with a click or words, he wasn't leaving Lacey alone.

Another click came through and Seth whispered. "I'm on the pickup guy."

Clicks came in response. Then Simpson grunted and Kyle wondered briefly if there was a third man.

. . .

Lacey stood at her opened car door and watched as Grayson Mitchell Jr. approached her. He was smiling, the rat, like he'd won a contest. "Ms. Burke."

"Grayson," she returned, not in the mood to give him any courtesy.

His smile faded and he raised his pistol. "You've been a lot of trouble, you know."

"Have I? Sorry. I thought I was just living my life, raising my son." She was surprised at the lack of fear in her voice, or in fact in her gut. She wasn't afraid of this man, she realized. Instead, she abhorred what he stood for, what he did. And the fact he had a gun pointed at her didn't faze her. That in and of itself warned her she needed to keep her wits about her.

"And you played with me, you bitch. If you'd sent the list and the picture when I first asked you to, I wouldn't have had to force you to do it."

"So, it was my fault?" She stepped away from her car, toward him.

"Hell yeah. What business is it of yours what I do? If your bastard of a lover hadn't gotten involved, hadn't put his nose in where it didn't belong, he'd still be here and you'd have popped out another mixed breed kid by now."

His sneer couldn't have been plainer and Lacey's temper rose. "You're nothing but a spoiled kid, aren't you?" She kept her voice cool and contemptuous. "Your daddy has been getting you out of scrapes your entire life. Is he going to get you out of this one too? When you shoot me is he going to say it was an accident? Or are you going to pin it on your buddies, like you tried to do when you wanted my son killed?"

His shot went wide and she darted around the back of the car and squatted behind the tire. Mitchell cursed and another shot rang out and a grunt followed. She peered around the tire and then moved to the end of the car. Another man stood beside Mitchell and someone was on the ground at the edge of the light. Lacey drew in a sharp breath as she took in the bearded chin. "Kyle," she whispered.

"What the hell you doing here," Mitchell ground out, his eyes darting around. The other man, skinny as a rail, held a pistol in one hand and a rifle in the other. Lacey groaned. It looked like the rifle Kyle had been preparing earlier in the day.

"You got some trouble, Mr. Mitchell. That guy was sneaking up on you." The skinny man's voice sounded tinny, almost as if he were speaking through a distortion device. Lacey ducked back at his nod toward her. "She had help."

"Well so did I. You got him?" Mitchell glanced around. "Where's Dean? Aren't you supposed to be covering the east side of the lot?"

"Dean's not at his spot. I looked. He's gone."

Skinny's head swiveled around, "There's more of 'em out there, Mr. Mitchell. Gotta be."

"You idiot. She brought her boyfriend. We knew she had someone with her at the motel. She's been shacked up with him for the last few days. And the other couple they were with is still there. The manager said so." Mitchell took a step toward the car and waved his pistol in Lacey's general direction. "Get out here, you bitch!"

She stood and took a step toward him, praying she'd be able to make it to Kyle. What had gone wrong?

When she stepped to the side of the car nearest Mitchell, he leveled the pistol at her and then said. "Shoot her."

She frowned then shot Skinny a look of surprise which he returned. "Me?"

"You. That's what I paid you for. Now, shoot her."

"But you said—"

"Fuck what I said! Shoot the bitch with her lover's rifle. It'll be perfect." Kyle was waving the pistol in the air wildly and Lacey wondered if he were high on his own product.

Skinny started to raise the gun when he collapsed into a heap, the gun dropping to the ground beside him. Lacey didn't think but lunged at Mitchell, her mind only on one thing. Kyle.

When she landed on top of him, Mitchell's hand

holding the gun flew up and another shot rang out. As Lacey landed on him, he cried out, then started hitting at her. She in turn took her fist and hit him in the temple, as Kyle had shown her earlier. While her force wasn't strong enough to disable the man, it would hurt enough to distract him, Kyle had said. Now, she put her full temper behind the blow and then, with a silent glee, reared up and put her knee into his groin. As she let her entire weight settle on her knee, she watched him pale and delighted in his scream.

She might have stayed there, grinding her knee into his balls if Boomer hadn't touched her shoulder. "I got him, Lacey. Go check on Kyle."

She scrambled to her feet and darted around Boomer, who flipped Mitchell to his stomach, then around Simpson who had Skinny on his belly as well. A small pool of blood was seeping out of Skinny somewhere and she stepped around it, her attention on Kyle.

She dropped to her knees, "Kyle? Kyle!"

He lay on his side, curled into a large ball, his hand covering his midsection. She laid her hand on his bearded cheek and said his name again before he opened his eyes.

"You okay?" He examined her with clear eyes, though his expression was tight with pain.

"Me? What about you? Where are you hurt?" She looked at the hand covering his stomach and swallowed. His fingers were stained, dark in the night.

"Stomach, I think."

She pulled her phone from her pants pocket and dialed 911 then turned back at him. "What can I do?"

"I'll be okay. Just give me a few days, I'll be fine." His voice faded and she swallowed against a sob as he closed his eyes.

THE ER'S waiting room was tiny, but then the hospital was too. Lacey paced the minuscule area. Saint and Celie stood at the edge of the room and Davey sat in one of the plastic-covered chairs, his dark brown eyes large and somber. "Mommy?"

"It's okay, sweetie. Mommy's okay." She turned to him and sat in the chair after picking him up. Her side twinged again, reminding her she'd stretched or strained something during the night.

"Car?" He held his current favorite car, the fire truck he and Kyle had been playing with the day before out to her. She accepted it with a smile and ran her thumb over the small wheels, turning them over and over.

When a scrub wearing doctor came through the doors, she stared up at him. "Anyone here for Richards?"

"Me, I am." Lacey shifted Davey to the seat and stood in front of the doctor. "How is he?"

"What's your relationship to Mr. Richards?" He asked, his exhaustion evident in his voice.

She thought about lying and saying she was his sister or his wife but when she opened her mouth, she merely said, "A friend."

He shook his head. "Sorry, I can't give you any information, privacy laws." He turned away only to stop when Agent Simpson came into the room and flashed his badge.

"He's involved in an investigation. Give me an update." Simpson stood square in the room while the doctor updated him, allowing their group to overhear.

"He's in surgery. We thought we'd have to transfer him to Seattle, but we have a decent surgeon here. So far, he's doing well. If you go to the surgical waiting room, they'll update you there." The doctor disappeared through the door and Lacey sat back, her heart pounding.

Surgery. He was in surgery and she hadn't known. When Celie came to a stop at her chair, she stood and held her hand out to Davey. "Let's go for a walk, honey."

"Potty?" Davey said and started doing his little dance that indicated he might have waited too late to make it. Lacey and Celie found the nearest bathroom and took care of that business and then hustled him as fast as his little legs would carry him to an equally tiny surgical waiting room.

The team took up the whole room, except for Seth who'd disappeared. Lacey thought that odd since he worked with Kyle but her attention soon became absorbed by the surgical nurse who apprised them that he was in recovery. The bullet had grazed his sleen and perforated his intestines, which increased the likelihood he'd get an infection. He'd be in the hospital for several days, if not weeks, but he'd pull through.

Lacey returned to her apartment, with Saint and Celie sleeping on the pull out couch again. When he spied his room, Davey ran around touching his toys as well as his race track comforter with awe, nearly bringing her to tears.

As she lay in the bed, Lacey thought of Kyle, of his actions when he'd heard the gunshots. He'd run headlong toward the action, toward the fire. For her. The night spread out before her, long and tedious, wakeful.

After a couple of hours of tossing and turning, she rose and dressed. When she nudged Celie on the shoulder, she had to jump back in a retreat to avoid getting hit.

"Sorry," Celie said and rubbed her eyes. "Anything wrong?"

Lacey shook her head, "I'm going back to the

hospital. Could you watch Davey for me? I'll try to be back before he wakes in the morning."

Celie's eyes widened at Lacey's request. "Is Kyle worse?"

"No. I just need to be there. Is it okay with you?"

"Sure. Take your time. We'll have pancakes in the morning," Celie grinned and lay back down. Saint snuffled beside her and rolled over.

Lacey drove through the predawn darkness, her mind on Kyle and her need to be near him. Even if he didn't wake, was never aware of her, she wanted to be beside him, to watch him breathe.

The hospital was nearly as silent as the roads, with the exception of occasional sounds of coughing, patients' alarms going off and personnel walking about. Lacey dodged a couple of technicians with rolling equipment that looked like they could run a space station. After learning his room number from a sleepy-looking nurse, Lacey snuck in only to see Agent Simpson seated in the one chair provided.

"How is he?" She whispered to the tall lean man in the rumpled jacket and tie.

"He's sleeping, hasn't been awake much since he came out of surgery." Simpson rubbed his chin, which was dark with stubble. "I didn't get a chance to ask if you're okay."

She waved her hand. "I'm fine. Where's Mitchell?"

Simpson smiled a shark's grin. "He's in federal custody. Started whining about being a senator's son as soon as we arrested him, but I think we've got enough on him to justify keeping him in custody for a while. You think you might be interested in testifying against him for kidnapping?"

She nodded enthusiastically then narrowed her eyes at the agent. "You aren't involved in the kidnapping case. It's out of your jurisdiction, isn't it?"

He nodded. "But I do know some FBI agents who are very interested in talking to you."

"And the drug charges?" She asked, her eyes on Kyle, who'd shifted in the bed.

"We're continuing to investigate that but with the photo and list you sent us, we should be able to connect Mitchell to the organization. That, combined with the fact that he was traveling in all of those areas on the dates listed, will be pretty good evidence that he's neck deep. The most compelling evidence will be you and your son."

She looked at the agent then bit her lip in understanding. "In other words, why would he go to the trouble of kidnapping Davey and trying to have me injured or killed if he wasn't involved."

"Exactly. Which is why it's important we connect the kidnapping and the extortion."

"Extortion my ass," the rough whisper carried from the bed clearly and both Lacey and Simpson turned to find Kyle watching them with bleary eyes. "The bastard tried to have her and Davey killed, Agent. Remember that."

Simpson approached the bed behind Lacey who'd hurried over to touch Kyle's hand. "Oh, I know. Extortion, coercion, murder for hire; we're planning on throwing every charge we can think of at the man. If for no other reason than to keep his team of attorneys busy while we get our ducks in a row."

"And your mole?"

"We're already working on that," Simpson said. "You going to be okay?"

"Yeah. Give me a few—"

"Weeks." Lacey interspersed before Kyle could narrow down the time. "He's going to have several weeks of recovery ahead of him, or at least that's what the nurse said, remember?" She looked at Kyle and squeezed his hand. "You took a pretty big chance out there."

"It was worth it," his eyes began to close though Lacey could tell he wanted to stay awake. He returned the squeeze and mumbled. "You going to be here when I wake up?"

She nodded through her tears, though she knew he couldn't see them. "I'll be here."

And she would. She knew, beyond all, that she'd be there for him. She would nurse him back to health, she'd follow him to wherever he lived and worked, and she'd raise her son beside him, if he'd have her. She'd take the chance on him and on loving him.

"Love you," he slurred, and she returned the sentiment before leaning down and kissing him to sleep.

The End

ACKNOWLEDGMENTS

My thanks to my Sprinting buddies. Writing is a lonely business and your encouragement and butt-kicking helped me finish this book. Here's to many more hours in Zoom!

Cover Art by Christine's Cover Creations

ABOUT KATE MCKEEVER

Kate McKeever was born and raised in the south and spent her childhood rambling in the woods and reading, often at the same time. She spent a lot of time in libraries as a volunteer and reader, then as a perennial student, so her mother thought. She tried several careers before settling down on her current one. Writing is a passion and joy. Kate loves to write about strong men and women finding love, even in the most trying times.

Website: www.katemckeever.net

Amazon: https://www.amazon.com/Kate-McKeever

OTHER BROTHERHOOD PROTECTOR
BOOKS BY KATE MCKEEVER

Saving Sidewinder

Sinner's Redemption

Saint's Fall

BROTHERHOOD PROTECTORS
ORIGINAL SERIES BY ELLE JAMES

Brotherhood Protectors Series

Montana SEAL (#1)

Bride Protector SEAL (#2)

Montana D-Force (#3)

Cowboy D-Force (#4)

Montana Ranger (#5)

Montana Dog Soldier (#6)

Montana SEAL Daddy (#7)

Montana Ranger's Wedding Vow (#8)

Montana SEAL Undercover Daddy (#9)

Cape Cod SEAL Rescue (#10)

Montana SEAL Friendly Fire (#11)

Montana SEAL's Mail-Order Bride (#12)

SEAL Justice (#13)

Ranger Creed (#14)

Delta Force Rescue (#15)

Dog Days of Christmas (#16)

Montana Rescue (Sleeper SEAL)

Hot SEAL Salty Dog (SEALs in Paradise)

Hot SEAL Hawaiian Nights (SEALs in Paradise)

Hot SEAL Bachelor Party (SEALs in Paradise)

ABOUT ELLE JAMES

ELLE JAMES also writing as MYLA JACKSON is a *New York Times* and *USA Today* Bestselling author of books including cowboys, intrigues and paranormal adventures that keep her readers on the edges of their seats. With over one hundred and eighty works in a variety of sub-genres and lengths she has published with Harlequin, Samhain, Ellora's Cave, Kensington, Cleis Press, and Avon. When she's not at her computer, she's traveling, reading or riding her ATV, dreaming up new stories. Learn more about Elle James at www.ellejames.com

Website | Facebook | Twitter | GoodReads | Newsletter | BookBub | Amazon

Follow Elle!
www.ellejames.com
ellejames@ellejames.com

facebook.com/ellejamesauthor
twitter.com/ElleJamesAuthor

Printed in Great Britain
by Amazon